# TIN SOLDIER

# SIGMUND BROUWER

# TIN SOLDIER

ORCA BOOK PUBLISHERS

**Library and Archives Canada Cataloguing in Publication**

Brouwer, Sigmund, 1959-, author
Tin soldier / Sigmund Brouwer.
(The seven sequels)

Issued in print and electronic formats.
ISBN 978-1-4598-0546-0 (pbk.).--ISBN 978-1-4598-0547-7 (pdf).--
ISBN 978-1-4598-0548-4 (epub)

I. Title.
PS8553.R68467T55 2014     jc813'.54     C2014-901541-0
C2014-901542-9

First published in the United States, 2014
**Library of Congress Control Number:** 2014935398

**Summary:** Webb puts his music career on hold while he searches for the truth about
his grandfather's role in the Vietnam War.

*Orca Book Publishers is dedicated to preserving the environment and has
printed this book on Forest Stewardship Council® certified paper.*

Orca Book Publishers gratefully acknowledges the support for its publishing
programs provided by the following agencies: the Government of Canada
through the Canada Book Fund and the Canada Council for the Arts,
and the Province of British Columbia through the BC Arts Council
and the Book Publishing Tax Credit.

Design by Chantal Gabriell
Cover photography by Shutterstock and Corbis Images, Dreamstime,
CGTextures and iStock
Author photo by Reba Baskett

One Tin Soldier—Words and Music by Dennis Lambert and Brian Potter
Copyright © 1969, 1974 SONGS OF UNIVERSAL, INC.
Copyright Renewed All Rights Reserved Used by Permission
Reprinted by permission of Hal Leonard Corporation

ORCA BOOK PUBLISHERS          ORCA BOOK PUBLISHERS
PO Box 5626, Stn. B                    PO Box 468
Victoria, BC Canada                     Custer, WA USA
v8R 6s4                                         98240-0468

www.orcabook.com
Printed and bound in Canada.

17  16  15  14  •  4  3  2  1

*To Eric, Shane, Ted, Richard, John and Norah.*
*Thanks for making the ride so much fun.*

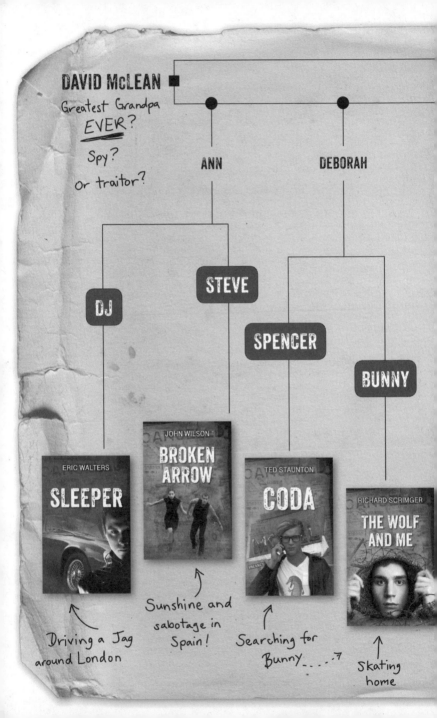

**DAVID McLEAN**
Greatest Grandpa
<u>EVER</u>?
Spy?
Or traitor?

ANN

DEBORAH

DJ

STEVE

SPENCER

BUNNY

ERIC WALTERS
**SLEEPER**

JOHN WILSON
**BROKEN ARROW**

TED STAUNTON
**CODA**

RICHARD SCRIMGER
**THE WOLF AND ME**

Driving a Jag
around London

Sunshine and
sabotage in
Spain!

Searching for
Bunny......⁊

Skating
home

MELANIE COLE

VERA McLEAN

CHARLOTTE    VICTORIA    SUZANNE

ADAM

WEBB

RENNIE

SIGMUND BROUWER
TIN SOLDIER

SHANE PEACOCK
DOUBLE YOU

NORAH McCLINTOCK
FROM THE DEAD

On the road in
the Deep South

Channeling
James Bond

Nazi-hunting
in Detroit

# READ THE ORIGINAL
# SEVEN (THE SERIES)
www.seventheseries.com

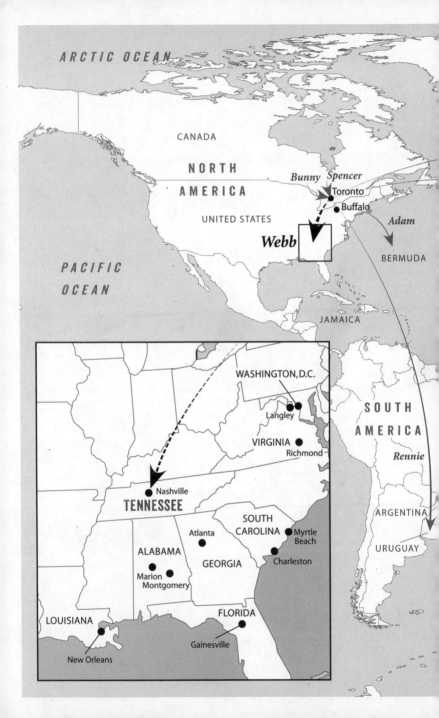

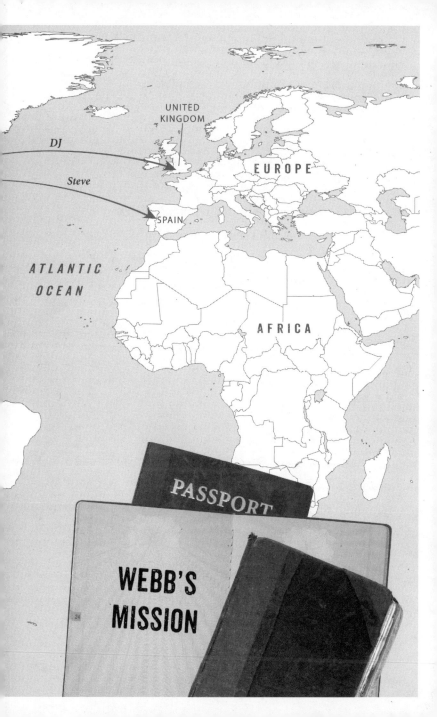

*There won't be any trumpets blowing*
*Come the judgment day,*
*On the bloody morning after*
*One tin soldier rides away.*

—FROM THE SONG "ONE TIN SOLDIER,"
BY DENNIS LAMBERT AND BRIAN POTTER

# ONE

Lying was wrong. Webb knew that.

Still, he wanted to lie to the old woman in front of him. Her name was Ruby Gavin, and he'd knocked on her front door, with flowers in hand, and spent about half an hour making pleasant small talk in her front parlor. It was just the two of them, late in the morning almost a week past Christmas. Webb sipped on his third teacup of hot cider, pretending to be hungry as he nibbled at her homemade shortbread cookies.

Ruby sat in her rocking chair across the parlor from Webb, a contented smile shaping the delicate wrinkles of her cheeks. A few wisps of fine white hair escaped the tight bun that was tied in place by a ribbon.

Webb had first met Ruby a few months earlier, here in her small hometown of Eagleville, Tennessee, some forty miles south of Nashville. Then she had been wearing a long dress with pink flowers against a white cotton background. Now her dress was dark brown and of a thicker material, with yellow and white flowers. Ruby was also wearing a heart-shaped ceramic pendant that hung from her neck on a gold chain.

Ruby had made the pendant when she was a little girl. She'd used the end of a wire to draw her initials on one side of the clay while it was still soft and damp, and on the other side she scratched the phrase *I love you forever, Daddy*. She had painted it with colored glazes, and after the teacher baked it in a kiln, she had given it to her daddy. When he'd gone off to war, he'd strung it on a gold chain and kept it close to his heart.

Webb knew this because he'd been the one to find it near a desolate trail in the Northwest Territories, and he'd been the one to return it to Ruby decades after her daddy had not come back from the war.

"Jim, I've sure enjoyed your company," Ruby said, "and you're so polite, it might take you another hour of listening to an old woman like me before you get around to what you want to ask, so let me help you out. Go ahead and tell me what's on your mind."

What was on his mind was a reunion with four of his six cousins the day after Christmas at their grandfather's cottage north of Toronto. The accidental discovery of a hidden compartment behind a log beside the fireplace. Fake passports, a mysterious notebook, cash in a dozen currencies and a Walther PPK pistol—James Bond's weapon of choice, as Spencer, one of his cousins, had pointed out.

"I was hoping you would introduce me to one of the veterans who attended your father's funeral," Webb told Ruby. "Someone who fought in Vietnam."

His answer wasn't technically a lie, but rather a deflection. Still, he felt a degree of guilt about deceiving Ruby Gavin. Webb drew a breath, waiting for the question that would force him to decide how much more of a lie he'd need to tell the old woman.

"I can do that," she said. "It's as easy as a phone call. Care to tell me why you need the introduction?"

This was the question he'd feared. Because he didn't want to explain. To her or to anyone else.

Not until he'd found out what he needed to about those passports and military identification cards.

Webb was ready with a lie. He'd planned to tell Ruby he was taking an online course to upgrade for university, that he was doing research for a paper on the Vietnam War.

He hesitated. Lying was wrong.

"I'd like it," he said, "if I didn't have to answer that."

"After all you've done for me, it's not my business to ask why you want help. I'm going to call Lee Knox right this minute. He's a stubborn man, but a good one, so try to look past his prickliness. Then I'm going to send you in his direction, but you're not leaving until you take a tin of shortbread cookies. Understand?"

"Understood." Food didn't interest him much these days, but Webb wasn't about to be rude.

"Tell me this though," Ruby said. "Are you in some kind of trouble? 'Cause if you are, I'll move heaven and earth to help you. It's the least I can do for you after you lifted the burden from me."

"No," Webb said. "I'm not in trouble."

That wasn't quite a lie, but close.

She cocked her head and examined him. He felt like flinching but didn't look away.

"Whatever it is," she said, "it's weighing heavy on you, isn't it?"

So heavy, Webb thought, it was almost enough to make him forget about the Nashville producer who had ripped him off a few months earlier. Who'd taken the songs Webb had recorded in his studio.

"I'll be okay," Webb said. And wondered if this was the real lie.

# TWO

It took Webb five minutes to walk to the one traffic light in Eagleville, where the post office sat kitty-corner to the town hall. Five minutes of thinking about the two military identification cards and the fake Canadian passport in the back pockets of his jeans.

From there, guided by Ruby's directions and the maps on his iPhone, Webb reached a turnoff for Cheatham Springs Road and kept walking. The road was a couple of miles of narrow pavement, up over the crest between two small valleys and partway down again, to where thickly wooded and winding gravel driveways led to houses screened by trees. That gave him plenty more time to think about the two laminated military ID cards and the two fake passports and why he was now looking for a mailbox with the name of a Vietnam veteran, Lee Knox, on it.

Both ID cards were on faded white stock with light blue borders, the words *ARMED FORCES OF THE UNITED STATES* printed in bold blue ink across the top. Some information on the cards, including a nine-digit military identification number, was typed. No computers back then. Hard to imagine a time when the Internet didn't exist.

The first card showed Private Jesse Lockewood's black-and-white photo, centered between two circular Army emblems, also in light blue ink. The photo showed a crew-cut soldier barely older than Webb. Even though it didn't list a birth date, the card had a typed expiry date: 23 March 1976. Lockewood would be in his mid-to-late-fifties now, about four decades older than Webb.

What was strange was that the photo on Private Jesse Lockewood's military card matched the photo on the other military card in Webb's back pocket. Except the other card had a different identification number and declared the same crew-cut soldier to be Corporal Benjamin Moody.

Both ID cards looked genuine, but obviously, unless the pictures were of twins, one man could not be two soldiers in the same army at the same time.

Something strange or even illegal had happened at the end of the Vietnam War that involved Jesse Lockewood and Benjamin Moody. Since Webb had found the cards with his grandfather's fake passports, it probably meant his grandfather had been been involved in the same illegal activity.

He didn't expect to find out everything from Lee Knox, but he had to start somewhere.

# THREE

Lee Knox was a widower with grown kids who lived in a clapboard house on the other side of the hill on Cheatham Springs Road. That's what Ruby Gavin had told Webb. When he admitted he didn't know what clapboard was, she told him it was the thin slats of wood that made up the siding. Any clapboard house these days was probably thirty or forty years old, because vinyl siding been around for years and didn't ever need painting. She said you could tell a lot about a person by how their clapboard looked.

As Webb walked up the long oak-lined driveway to Lee's house, a mockingbird—the size of a robin, gray with flashes of white in its tail—hopped along in front of him. The mockingbird finally got tired of Webb and flew away, and Webb reached a wide clearing from which he could see Knox's white clapboard house. It was on a hillside, overlooking the valley to the south. Beside the house was a double garage with its doors up, revealing a large motorcycle with gleaming chrome and an older, bright red Camaro. The two-story house was large, with two rocking chairs on a wide front porch and an American flag waving in the breeze. The clapboard was freshly painted, matching the clapboard on the exterior of the garage. If Ruby was right about clapboard houses revealing things about their owners, Lee Knox was a person who took good care of things and cared about details.

The flower beds in front of the house confirmed Webb's impression. He stepped onto the porch and was about to knock when the door opened, and the large man in the doorway studied Webb through round, frameless glasses. He had a few wrinkles, and the beginning of jowls under his close-cropped beard. The man's hair was shaved so short that the coal-black skin of his head contrasted sharply with the gray stubble.

He was wearing sweatpants and an orange jersey that said *UT*. University of Tennessee. Now there was some major branding. Webb saw those letters everywhere in Nashville, on everything from bumper stickers to coffee cups.

The man in front of Webb held a magazine, as if Webb had interrupted his reading.

"Hello," Webb said. "My name is Jim Webb."

"Why are you here?"

"Because Ruby Gavin—"

"I know Ruby Gavin sent you here. She called, asked me if I would mind somebody coming by to ask me a few questions about the army and Vietnam. What I want to know is what questions you have. More to the point, I want to know why you put garbage down at my mailbox as you walked up."

"Garbage?" Webb asked.

"Garbage. I've got a surveillance camera on my driveway. It showed you clear as day putting something down and walking away. Makes me wonder, too, why you'd park your car somewhere on the road and walk in like some long-haired punk trying to sneak up on me."

*Long-haired punk?* Webb wanted to punch the guy. Normally, he could handle insults, but for the last while, he'd been getting angry at little things that usually didn't bother him. "I don't have a car," Webb said, forcing a flatness into his voice as he swallowed the anger. "And what I put down by the mailbox is the same thing I'm going to pick up on my way back. A tin of cookies that Ruby baked for me. I set it down because I thought it might look strange knocking on your door with cookies, and I didn't want to have to explain them."

The answer softened Lee's face a bit. "An old gal like Ruby bakes you cookies, that tells me something else, doesn't it?"

So does freshly painted clapboard, Webb thought, and a perfect flower garden even though the flowers and bushes won't be in bloom until spring. *It tells a person something.* So when could you believe what it told you and when couldn't you?

Lee pointed at a rocking chair. "We might as well sit. You want tea?"

Webb had been in the south long enough to know that Lee meant iced tea. Down here, if you wanted it hot, you had to ask for hot tea. In Canada, when you ordered tea, unless you said iced tea, it came hot and steeped. More than once, he'd wished Tim Hortons would set up in Nashville.

"Yes, please," Webb said. "Unsweetened."

That was the other thing. You had to make sure you said unsweetened, or it would be so thick with sugar it was hard to drink. Webb had already filled up on cider, but tea wouldn't hurt. He'd just have to make sure he used the bathroom before getting on a bus back to Nashville.

"Then set yourself down," Lee said. "I'll be back."

Lee took a half step and paused, looking at Webb's shirt, and said, "Saskatchewan Roughriders. College team?"

"CFL," Webb said. In Nashville, if he wasn't wearing his usual black T-shirt, Webb liked to wear different CFL shirts. He liked being reminded of Canada when he looked in the mirror. Today it was green and white—*Go Riders*. The T-shirt had been a real find, only five dollars from a surly ten-year-old at a garage sale in Toronto.

"CFL?"

"Canadian Football League."

"They play on skates?" Lee asked, chuckling.

Webb sat in one of the rocking chairs and leaned back, thinking about what Lee had called him. *Long-haired punk.* Yes, he was mad at Lee for judging him because he had long hair, but if Webb was being honest with himself, it had not occurred to him that Lee Knox might be black. Maybe there was a good song in this somewhere, about making snap judgments. *If* Webb felt like writing a song. He was in Nashville for that reason, but the well had been dry for weeks. He didn't seem to have the energy for it anymore, not since getting ripped off.

Lee came onto the porch with two tall glasses of tea, ice cubes clinking as he walked.

"Warm for December," Lee said. "This is the first time since Christmas I've been able to enjoy sitting on the porch."

Webb was used to snowy Christmases, so any day in December in Nashville seemed warm.

"How did you get here?" Lee asked. *Get* sounded like *git.* The entire sentence sounded like *howdjew git heah.*

"I'm from the Toronto area," Webb explained. "I flew down to Nashville. I would have skated, but the ice ran out south of Buffalo."

Lee raised an eyebrow.

Gotcha, Webb thought.

"What I meant," Lee said, "was how did you get here today? Ruby told me you were living in Nashville. It's a long ways to walk."

"Bus," Webb said.

"That wouldn't have been easy."

"With connections, about four hours," Webb said.

"Four hours' travel to come and ask some questions," Lee said. "Must be important."

More important than he was going to reveal to Lee. So Webb's answer was to reach into his back pocket and pull out the pieces of military ID. One face. Two different names.

# FOUR

"Hang on," Lee said, putting up a hand to stop Webb from passing the cards to him. "Ruby said you wanted to talk to me about Vietnam, ask some questions about a soldier there."

Webb nodded. "I was at her father's funeral—played a couple of songs in his honor. She said some local Vietnam vets attended out of respect, because he'd been in the military too. She said you were one of them."

"Yes, I was at the funeral," Lee said. "I remember thinking that kids these days hadn't earned the right to wear their hair long like you do."

Earned the right to wear long hair? What kind of stupid thing was that to say? Webb thought. Maybe adults these days hadn't earned the right to criticize kids they didn't know. Especially since Lee Knox had no idea why Webb refused to cut his hair. Webb fought an irrational impulse to stand and fight.

"I remember thinking that even though I didn't like the way you looked," Lee continued, "you sounded good on that guitar. Okay. Better than good."

And maybe I don't care about your opinion and maybe I don't like orange jerseys with *UT* in big letters, Webb thought. What business was it of Lee's how Webb dressed and looked? But Webb needed information, and again he reminded himself there was no sense starting an argument.

"I told Ruby I'd hear you out as a favor to her," Lee said. "But I might be the wrong person for you to ask about the conflict."

Yeah, Webb thought, if you don't like kids because of how they look, you might be the wrong person for anybody. But he kept that to himself as well.

Instead, he said, "You fought in Vietnam, right?"

"I served in Vietnam, son. I served my country and I served the people of my country. And since it's apparent you don't understand the difference between fighting and serving, I think you are proving my point. Which is this: I might be the wrong person for you to ask for help."

"Help me understand the difference then. You were a solider. You had to fight, right?"

"That war was only forty or so years ago. I flew home in my uniform, and as I walked through the airport, people spat on me and called me a baby killer. Do you know why?"

"No," Webb said. "I don't."

"Do you know why the war was started?"

"No," Webb said. "I don't."

"Do you know why the war was lost?"

"No," Webb said. "I don't."

"When did it start? When did it end? Who was president at the start? Who was president at the end? What happened at Kent State? Who shot Martin Luther King Jr. and why?"

Webb didn't answer any of the questions. He didn't even speak. He suspected it would be a weak excuse to say he didn't know because he wasn't American.

"See"—Lee drew a deep breath—"we've got a generation of kids who know nothing about what shaped my generation. In Vietnam, I held friends as they died in my arms. I've got other friends came back with me, missing an arm or a leg, who didn't want to fight but were willing to serve. These are lessons we paid for in blood, son. I deeply resent the fact that these lessons are already forgotten, and that's why I may not be the person you want to speak to about Vietnam. Because when it comes to Vietnam, I'm an angry person." Lee paused and evaluated Webb. "You still want to ask your questions? Like you're working on some report for school?"

Webb didn't shy from the man's hard gaze. He'd faced worse. Way worse. "So you're telling me I need to know the history, but I shouldn't ask any questions about it. From a person who was there."

Lee looked at Webb for about thirty seconds, then snorted. "You put it like that, it makes me feel some-what foolish." He continued, "I'm aware that you did something wonderful for Ruby by bringing word to her about her father's disappearance. I understand you faced down a bear in the process."

"Yes," Webb said, not adding any details. It had been part of Webb's time in the wilderness of the North. A mission for his grandfather that had helped him uncover something for Ruby Gavin. Webb's business wasn't anyone else's business, especially not the business of a guy who thought it was funny to suggest that Canadians played football on skates.

When Lee realized Webb wasn't going to say anything more, he held out his hand for the ID cards. "Everyone around here is glad you helped her. She's a good woman. What is it you want to know?"

Webb handed him the card with the name Jesse Lockewood.

Lee studied it. "Seeing a card like this brings back memories. I still have my card, somewhere."

Webb handed him the second card, with the same photo that identified the man as Benjamin Moody.

"Interesting," Lee said. "A little bit of fraud going on here."

Then he snorted, as if Webb were an idiot. "You think maybe somehow, out of 100,000 grunts serving at the time, I know this guy?"

The guy expected attitude, Webb could give him attitude. "I'm from Canada. I meet people here and tell them I'm from Toronto, and they tell me they know someone in Vancouver and ask if I know that person too. It's a forty-hour drive across the country to Vancouver. So no, I'm not thinking you know this guy. I was hoping you might know someone who might know someone who might know how to track him down."

"Did you wake up in a bad mood?" Lee asked. "Or are you like this all the time?"

"Nope," Webb said. He'd let Lee figure out the implications. Although it did seem that Webb was always waking up in a bad mood these days.

"As a favor to Ruby," Lee said, "I can find the right government office for you to start asking questions. You can take your bad mood there."

Webb had no intention of doing that. If his search went through official channels, maybe it would lead to the wrong person asking the wrong questions about his grandpa, and it might turn out that the man he had loved was a spy. If that information went public, it could hurt a lot of people. No way was Webb going to say any of this out loud. He could barely say it to himself.

Webb stood. "Mr. Knox, I sure appreciate your time. And I think you are right. You are the wrong person to ask about this."

"Sit down," Lee said. "Somehow we got started off on the wrong foot. If it's my fault, I apologize. I'm not averse to asking around. And I'm not averse to minding my own business about it. As I said, Ruby Gavin is a good woman, and I know what you did for her was a big help."

Webb remained standing. *Despite my long hair?* he wanted to say. Webb wasn't sure he liked Lee Knox. But it didn't matter. Webb would be down the driveway in a minute or two.

"My insurance business doesn't take much of my time these days," Lee said. "My wife, bless her soul, has passed away. My children are grown, and except for golf and tending to my flower bed, there's not a lot happening in my life. You've got me curious enough that I don't mind asking around, but I'd rather make you a deal than do this for nothing."

Webb sat again. If he didn't start here, where else could he start? He didn't know anybody in the military.

"I need some parts from Montgomery for my Camaro," Lee said. "That's about two hundred and fifty miles south of here, straight down the interstate.

How about you pick up those parts for me, and when you get back, I'll tell you what I've learned. Because yes, I have a few friends who might be able to help us track down this soldier, and while you're gone, I'll make those calls."

"I don't have a car, so it might take me awhile," Webb said, calculating how he'd do it. Probably by Greyhound. It was going to cost him the bus fare, but he could pack sandwiches in case he got hungry, and that would make it as inexpensive as possible. It was money he couldn't afford to spend, but if there was a chance it would help clear his grandfather, he'd spend it.

"You're thinking bus, right?" Lee said. "I'll cover the cost of the ticket and meals and even a night's stay, if you need it. Plus I'll pay you for your time. We'll trade cell numbers. You'll be looking for Jimmie Lee Jackson, and after you find him, send me a text."

Webb wondered if he needed to be suspicious about the offer.

"Cash up front," Lee said. "Hundred bucks for your time, and all expenses covered. I know someone who can tell me if either of those cards is fake, so leave them with me and I'll check with my contacts and ask some questions. With luck, when you get back, I'll have some answers for you."

It might not lead anywhere, Webb thought, but it beat sitting alone in his apartment and trying to find the energy to write a song that he doubted would get cut anywhere anyhow.

# FIVE

At 4:00 PM, a little more than twenty-four hours after walking away from Lee Knox, Jim Webb stepped out of a taxi at 400 Washington Avenue in Montgomery, Alabama, to get Camaro parts from a man named Jimmie Lee Jackson.

Immediately, he wondered if he'd got something wrong.

Webb's total travel time for the day had been nine hours, his luggage a guitar travel bag with a small outer pouch. Webb had rolled toothpaste and a toothbrush into a clean T-shirt and tucked it in the pouch. That was all he'd anticipated needing for an overnight trip. As the bus had rolled up and down the gentle hills and around the equally gentle curves going south on Interstate 65, Webb had played softly on his travel guitar, trying to shake off another day and another bad mood.

The guitar was a Baby Taylor, the wood a natural soft brown. Unlike his Gibson J-45, which was acoustic, the smaller travel guitar had a built-in pickup for a quarter-inch jack and cable. Webb could plug it into an amp, of course, but the real reason for the pickup was that he could plug his cable into an input device for his iPhone. That meant he could strum the guitar and listen to the music through his earbuds, and practice in almost complete silence. These days, though, he felt more like hitting the strings hard on a cheap, shiny black electric he'd purchased from a pawnshop. Nothing like a little heavy metal to brighten the day. Trouble was, the electric wasn't a good travel guitar. And if Webb wasn't playing guitar, it was like he wasn't breathing.

As he looked around, sunset was less than an hour away. Webb didn't have much time to find Jimmie Lee Jackson if he was going to find a motel before dark.

Webb felt a growing confusion. A bunch of elementary-school kids were lining up behind a few teachers, obviously getting ready to leave on a yellow bus. Schoolkids? Not what he associated with car parts.

The address Lee had given him was not for a house or apartment or business. It was a monument of some kind. There was a huge circular black-granite table with water emerging from a hole in the center and flowing evenly across the top and down the sides. Behind the circular table was a black-granite wall, curved outward like a dam. Etched on the granite wall was an inscription easy to read from the sidewalk where Webb had stepped out of the taxi.

> *... Until justice rolls down like waters*
> *and righteousness like a mighty stream*
> *—Martin Luther King Jr.*

That would be a cool hook to a song, Webb thought, if he ever felt like tinkering with lyrics again. He kept turning his head to search for Jimmie Lee Jackson. Behind the circular granite table and the curved granite wall was a three-story building with large black reflective windows.

Webb double-checked his iPhone, glancing at a photo on the screen. He'd taken a snapshot of the sheet of paper Lee Knox had given him. Easy to lose a sheet of paper, but if he took a snapshot and uploaded it to the cloud, it would always be available.

The handwriting on the photo hadn't changed; Webb had not made a mistake. The note said, *Jimmie Lee Jackson, 400 Washington Ave., Montgomery, AL. He'll be out front, easy to find.*

The schoolkids marched in formation toward yellow buses down the road, and that left Webb alone with some middle-aged women who were running their fingers along the top of the granite circle.

Webb moved closer, curious to see why they were doing that. Etched in lines around the edge of the circle were dates and names.

18 • AUG • 1965 JONATHAN DANIELS • SEMINARY STUDENT KILLED BY DEPUTY • HAYNESVILLE, AL

18 • JUL • 1965 WILLIE WALLACE BREWSTER • KILLED BY NIGHTRIDERS • ANNISTON, AL

9 · JUL · 1965 CONGRESS PASSES VOTING RIGHTS ACT OF 1965

Webb looked for more clues to understanding what it was all about. The sign on the nearby building said *Civil Rights Memorial Center.*

Not much help there. He was here to pick up car parts. Had Lee Knox called Jimmie Lee Jackson and told him to wait all day at this spot for a kid with long hair and a guitar?

That made no sense.

Webb pulled out his iPhone and sent a text to Lee Knox. No sign of Jimmie Lee Jackson. And address doesn't look like a place to pick up car parts.

He put the device back in his pocket. People were running their fingers along the etchings, beneath the thin sheet of water that flowed perfectly in all directions from the center.

Webb found himself doing the same, reading with a sense of outrage the names and descriptions etched on the granite table as the water flowed around his fingertips.

He read about Virgil Lamar Ware. Thirteen years old. Riding the handlebars of his brother's bicycle when he was shot by white teenagers who had come from a segregationist rally held after the bombing of the Sixteenth Street Baptist Church.

Segregation? Didn't that mean separating blacks from whites? One of the questions Lee Knox had asked the day before came back to Webb: *Who shot Martin Luther King Jr. and why?*

Webb walked in a circle, reading the inscriptions in the silence.

Then he saw a familiar name: Jimmie Lee Jackson.

26 · FEB · 1965 JIMMIE LEE JACKSON · CIVIL RIGHTS MARCH · KILLED BY STATE TROOPER · MARION, AL

This was the purpose of the note? Webb pulled out his iPhone and looked at the photo of the note again. *Jimmie Lee Jackson, 400 Washington Ave., Montgomery, AL. He'll be out front, easy to find.*

As Webb stared back and forth between the iPhone and the etched letters, someone spoke behind him.

"Hey, man, you Jim Webb?"

Webb turned. The speaker was about six inches shorter than Webb. Asian. Mid-fifties. Wispy black mustache that looked like it had been dyed to keep out the gray. Jeans, leather jacket.

"I'm Jim Webb." One word flashed through Webb's mind: *Vietnam*. And for that reason, his instincts made him suspicious.

"Trong Ti." The speaker extended his right hand, and although Webb was still trying to figure things out, he instinctively reached out as well.

As Trong's hand pulled away from the sleeves of the leather jacket, Webb saw tattooed symbols on Trong's forearm. A coffin. Three candles. And initials: BTK.

Gang symbols? Webb's suspicion deepened.

"Lee Knox said I could meet you here," Trong said. "Glad I found you."

Trong pointed at a black Cadillac with tinted windows, parked illegally just down the street, hazards flicking on and off. "We've got a meeting set up at a restaurant for you. Hope you like Italian food."

"Great," Webb said. He'd been sent to get car parts. "And you've got the painting Lee wants me to get for his collection?"

"All wrapped up and ready," Trong said, flashing a smile. "Hope you're hungry. It's a great restaurant."

Yeah, a painting. That was all Webb needed to confirm that it would be a big mistake to get into the Caddy with tinted windows.

He wondered about options. Walk over and join the women behind him at the memorial? No, if something bad was happening, that would put them in danger.

Just bolt?

Call 9-1-1?

None of the options sounded good.

The sound of a revving motorcycle distracted both of them as it pulled over to the curb only a few steps away.

It was a big bike—not a Harley, but around the same size. Gleaming chrome engine. Vibrant red fender skirts covering the tires. Rich leather seat with a chrome bar at the back. Saddlebags. Image of an eagle wing painted on the gas tank.

The rider, who wore black leather pants and a black leather jacket, flipped up the visor of a stars-and-stripes helmet. Long dark hair flowed out beneath the helmet, and the face that appeared was definitely female. As in good-looking female. About Webb's age.

"Webby," she said. "Sorry I'm late for our date! Let's get going. The movie starts in ten minutes."

There was a spare helmet snapped to the side of the rumbling motorcycle. She unclipped it and held it out.

Webb weighed his options: a Cadillac with ominous tinted windows driven by a guy who might be a Vietnamese gangster, or a cool-looking motorcycle, definitely ridden by a beautiful girl. He'd have to wrap his arms around her waist and hold on tight.

Not a difficult decision.

Webb glanced down at his iPhone to thumb it to the camera app. He lifted it and took a quick snapshot of the face of the man in front of him.

"Hey!" Trong said.

"Got to run," Webb said.

Guitar bag slapping against his back, he jumped on the bike.

# SIX

The girl gunned the motorcycle before he could get his helmet on, forcing him to hold the helmet in his right hand and wrap his left arm around her waist. She almost immediately did a U-turn as Trong dashed to the Cadillac. Her move to dodge a semi-truck heading toward them raised Webb's heart rate by about a thousand beats a minute. She turned into an alley, waited for him to put the helmet on, then, without answering any of his questions, gunned the big motorcycle again, so hard that he needed to hang on with both arms to keep from falling. With survival the only thing on his mind, Webb didn't give much thought to the whole hanging-on-to-a-beautiful-girl-on-a-motorcycle thing. He wouldn't have cared if he was clutching a bearded man who hadn't showered in three weeks. He just wanted the pavement to stop blurring, especially through the turns.

The ride slowed down some, and with dusk almost on them, the dark-haired girl idled the motorcycle through the gates of a junkyard patrolled by roaming rottweilers. Webb wondered if maybe he should have chosen the Cadillac and the possible gangster.

When she stopped the motorcycle in front of a shack between two large stacks of smashed and compressed junk cars, Webb wanted to go back to the blurry pavement. Might be good to be on a highway again, since the three rottweilers were moving in fast.

The girl jumped from the motorcycle and pulled off her helmet. As she shook her hair loose, Webb saw that she was wearing a Bluetooth device around her ear.

As the dogs approached, she commanded, "Sit. Any closer and I'll rip your heads off."

All three stopped and whined.

"Just joking," she said. She set the helmet on the motorcycle and knelt. "Come here, boys."

She scratched their heads, and they rolled like puppies for her.

Webb stood and stretched his legs. His guitar travel bag was still strapped to his back. He pulled off his helmet and set it on the motorcycle. He was in the type of bad mood that came from not understanding what was happening.

He gave the motorcycle a closer look. What he'd thought was an eagle wing on the gas tank was the head of someone who could have been an Apache chief, and the feathers that flowed back in the shape of a wing were the chief's headdress.

"That's a 1946 Indian Chief," she said to Webb's back. "Seventy-four-cubic-inch flathead."

"Wow," Webb said, turning to her. Even in the last light of the day, it was difficult not to get lost in a face that could have been on the cover of a fashion magazine. "Someone measured his skull?"

"Huh?"

"And calling him a flathead Indian is racist, wouldn't you say?" It felt good to vent his dark mood, especially since she hadn't realized he'd been mocking her.

"Indian Chief is the name of the motorcycle," she said in the tone of voice that made it clear she thought Webb was an idiot. "Flathead is the type of engine."

"Good thing you told me," Webb said, "or I would have never figured it out."

"Like you didn't figure out that the raised bar behind the seat is for the passenger to hold on to?"

"I'm not an idiot," Webb said.

"Then why didn't you use it instead of holding on to me all the way?"

"I'm not an idiot," Webb repeated.

"Oh, I get it," she said. "Because you wanted the thrill of holding onto a g-i-r-l? Or is spelling it out too complicated for you?"

"At least you got the g-i-r-l remark. You missed the one about measuring the chief's skull."

She cocked her head, as if replaying their conversation.

"Nuts," she said with a sudden grin. "I did miss it, didn't I? And that wasn't a bad joke, now that I think about it."

It was a grin that made Webb want to roll over like the rottweilers.

"Cool motorcycle," Webb said. "I'm not going to be surprised if you're the one who restored it."

He'd said it as a peace offering of sorts.

She didn't take it that way. "So now you're trying to prove you're not a jerk who makes stereotypical assumptions about women?"

He fired back, "Just like you're trying to prove you're not a dumb girl and can see right through my feeble attempt at a compliment?"

With a hand on her hip and her head cocked, she studied Webb for a few moments. "Not bad. We just might get along."

"Telling me who you are and what happened back at the Civil Rights Memorial would go a long ways toward that," Webb answered.

"I'm just a delivery girl," she said. She pointed at the shack. Lights were on behind the windows. "He's waiting for us."

# SEVEN

The inside of the shack was tidier and more luxurious than Webb expected. It was about the size of a school classroom. The roof and exterior walls of the shack were covered in sheets of tin, but the interior was smooth, clean drywall, painted brown, and a brown linoleum floor. Framed photographs of the girl filled one wall, some of them showing her in dirt-bike competitions. A second wall had photos of restored motorcycles, including the 1946 Indian Chief Webb had just ridden on, and a third wall displayed photos of soldiers in uniform. The fourth wall consisted of windows that overlooked the junkyard.

Filing cabinets lined one wall, and a huge desk sat in the middle of the room. The computer monitor was angled so that the person at the desk could look at the computer screen but still have a clear view out the window. The desk had a couple of chairs in front of it. The surface of the desk was bare except for a single sheet of paper. Behind the desk, leaning back with hands clasped behind his head, sat a man with a long, ragged gray beard and matching thick, ragged hair.

He wore a T-shirt with the sleeves cut off, and his biceps were massive. Snake tattoos wrapped around both of his arms. The T-shirt fit tightly, but not because the man was flabby. He might have been in his late fifties or early sixties, but Webb decided the man could probably still win a wrestling match against a bear.

"Jim Webb," the man said. Statement. Not a question.

Webb nodded.

"Blue Bombers," the man said. He had a soft voice. "Air force?"

"Football," Webb said. Today's T-shirt was the Winnipeg Blue Bombers. Manitoba. Middle of the country. Forty-below winters and summers so filled with mosquitoes you wished the blizzards would return. The Bombers were sometimes east division and sometimes west division. Ten-time Grey Cup winners. Grey Cup. Not Super Bowl. Super Bowl was a party with some great football. Grey Cup was an endurance event with great football and three opponents on the field—two teams and brutal weather.

The man leaned forward to take the tilt out of his chair and rose easily to his feet. He reached across and extended a hand. Webb shook it and decided the man could use his hands to tear a fender off a junker car.

The man pointed at the chairs in front of his desk. "Feel like sitting while we talk?"

Webb sat. With reluctance.

"Ali?" the man said as he took his chair.

She took the other chair.

Webb waited.

"I'm Roy Hawkins," the man said. "And you've met my daughter, Ali."

Daughter. Webb thought it was a good thing she didn't get her looks from her dad. Not the thing to mention though.

Webb waited. Roy already knew his name, so Webb didn't have to introduce himself.

Roy said, "Are you actually as calm as you look?"

"Don't like talking about my feelings," Webb said. "Don't like people playing games with me either. I figured I'd listen to what this was about, and then I would go on my way."

"Might not be that easy," Roy said. "Because someone has started a war. Maybe I don't look angry, but you should know I'm ready to start ripping off heads, and you're going to help me find the people with those heads still attached."

"I might not look angry either," Webb said, "but someone just sent me on a nine-hour wild-goose chase to read a name on a memorial. A guy who lied by saying I was on my way to get parts for a Camaro. And I'm not real good at being told what to do. So if you want help, asking works a lot better."

Roy gave that some thought. "Fair enough. I don't like being told what to do either."

"And if you've been talking to Lee," Webb continued, "then you're the one with parts for his '72 Camaro. If so, I hope the parts are small enough to fit right where I'm going to tell him to—"

"My daughter is beside you," Roy said. "I'd prefer the conversation remain polite."

"If he offends me, Daddy," Ali said, "I'll take care of it myself. Not that your language is perfect. Think I didn't hear your telephone call with Lee this morning?"

Roy smiled sweetly at Ali. "I can use those words in front of you because I know you've never heard them before and you don't know what they mean."

"Of course, Daddy," she said. "Absolutely."

Webb had his phone out, looking down at it and ignoring the conversation.

Roy spoke to Webb, now with a touch of anger. "Son, it drives me crazy when people check their phones in the middle of a conversation."

Webb didn't lift his head. He'd done a quick Google search and the results were just coming up.

"Son," Roy said. Now there was a real edge to his voice. "So far you've made a good impression. Don't ruin it."

Ali reached from her chair and put her hand on Webb's arm. "Really. You should listen. Nobody likes it when Roy gets mad."

Webb kept scanning his screen.

"Son!" Roy slammed a fist on the desk.

Webb started reading in silence.

"Son!" Roy slammed the desk harder.

Webb had seen enough on the screen. As if the fist slams had not happened, Webb slid the phone across to Roy. "I think you should look at this."

Roy's jaw might have been clenched, but the beard hid it. But his upper face was tight, as if he was debating whether to lecture Webb again.

Webb cut him off. "You don't scare me, okay? So quit trying to push me around. You want my help, I've already started. It's on the phone."

Roy grunted and pushed the phone toward Ali without looking at the screen.

Ali said, "Daddy needs reading glasses. He hates wearing them with strangers around."

"Ruins the whole snake-tattoo, tough-guy biker look?" Webb asked Roy.

"Roy," Ali said, "this guy has a sense of humor. I like that."

Webb hadn't been trying to be funny. It was just part of his bad mood.

"I don't," Roy growled at Webb, but Webb could tell that Roy had wanted to laugh at Webb's shot at him.

Ali took the phone. She read for a few moments, then said, "Born to kill."

"That was a phrase soldiers had on their helmets in 'Nam," Roy said.

"But this is about a gang," Ali said, holding up the phone. "He just googled *tattoo* and *BTK* and *coffin* and *candles*. It came up with a Wiki article about a Vietnamese street gang based out of New York."

Roy shifted his gaze to Webb.

"Lee told you I'd be at the memorial," Webb said. "That's easy to figure out. I can even guess he was trying to teach me something by sending me to the memorial—"

"Let me tell you," Roy interrupted. "He said you had attitude, but he must have seen something in you that he liked if he cared enough to send you there on a detour. Lee's a good man."

"He told me to send him a text from the memorial. That way, he could let you know that I was there. So you or Lee sent Ali to pick me up there and bring me here for the car parts. How am I doing so far?"

"Almost right," Roy said. "Ali was waiting there the entire time, looking for you to show up."

"What I can't understand," Webb said, "is how a guy from a Vietnamese gang knew I'd be there and who I was. Unless you or Lee told him. But if that was the case, Ali wouldn't have needed to get me out of there. So I don't think you or Lee sent him there. Which leaves me some questions. How did he know I'd be there? How did he know who I was? And what did he want?"

"Those are my questions too," Roy said. "Lee and I wondered if someone would show up. Ali was there to wait until someone moved in on you and see who it might be."

"You were using me as bait."

"You were safe. Ali was there."

Webb thought of the semi that had almost run them over when Ali did a U-turn on the motorcycle. Safe.

"You were using me as bait," Webb said again.

His anger must have come out in his voice, because Roy grinned and repeated Webb's words back to him. "You don't scare me, okay? So quit trying to push me around."

"Why were you using me as bait?" A joke from Roy wasn't going to improve Webb's mood.

"Last night," Roy said, "someone burned down Lee's house and his garage. To the ground. I'd say at this point, it's looking like all this is happening because of the questions Lee asked about those identification cards you gave him."

# EIGHT

Two hours later, Ali swung the big rumbling motorcycle into a parking spot in front of a small café on
the main street of a small town. She didn't turn off the
engine. She didn't get off the motorcycle.

Webb did. He set his helmet on the passenger seat
of the bike. He groaned and stretched his legs. Then
his back. They had gone about eighty miles on the
Indian Chief, every mile at the speed limit because
they couldn't risk being entered into a computer for
a traffic violation.

As Webb completed his stretching, Ali snapped
the spare helmet back into its strap.

"Delivery complete," Ali said, her words nearly lost in the deep throb of the idling engine. "Good luck."

"Yeah, thanks for—"

Webb stopped, because he was speaking to exhaust fumes. She'd dropped the bike into gear and roared away from the curb. She was beautiful but obviously a pain. He told himself not to think about how her smile gave him the same boost as, say, a sunrise or a good song.

Webb checked out his surroundings. The sign at the town limit had read *Welcome to Historic Marion Est. 1817 "The College City."* She'd taken him straight downtown, past brick two-story buildings with advertisements painted directly onto the brick. He hadn't seen a college.

In front of him was Mack's Café, with a small neon light inside the window that glowed *OPEN*.

So, Webb thought, alone in a strange place. Again.

Webb was accustomed to solitude. He was accustomed to taking care of himself. About a year ago, he'd been living on the streets. Still, it was unsettling to find himself in this situation. He had his travel bag with his guitar inside it, a hundred bucks cash, give or take, and a debit card for maybe six hundred bucks in savings.

That was all he needed, right? He could walk away, find a sheltered bus stop to sleep in overnight, and find a way back to Nashville, where he would work on new songs.

Or he could step inside the café and get more involved in something that had already resulted in arson and maybe attempted murder.

Webb knew what he wanted to choose. A sheltered bus stop.

But his grandfather, David McLean, had made it possible for Webb to get to Nashville in the first place. Webb owed a lot to his grandfather and to his memory. Webb had no choice but to try to clear his grandfather's name.

What if stepping inside the café only confirmed the worst about David McLean? He pushed aside the troubling thought.

Webb told himself to trust his grandfather, the man he believed had done nothing wrong. Webb pushed open the door to the café. Sitting in a booth at the back was Lee Knox.

Webb slid into the booth across from Lee.

"Hungry?" Lee asked. There was a leather jacket folded on the seat beside him, and he was wearing a UT sweatshirt. "I'm buying. I suggest the meatloaf."

Webb wasn't that hungry, but he nodded. Lee waved over the waitress, who took their order in silence. Webb ordered meatloaf. He was irritated with Lee, so it made him feel better to make the man pay for food that Webb wasn't going to enjoy.

"How was the ride?" Lee asked after the waitress left. "Lots of turns, like she was lost?"

"Lots of fast turns," Webb said. "Like someone was chasing us."

"Good," Lee said. "Roy and I are acting on the assumption that people are going to try to track us. Ali was supposed to make sure she wasn't followed."

"People?" Webb asked. How crazy was this? "What people?"

"Don't know yet," Lee said. "Need to find out."

"People who can track us through, say, traffic violations?"

"We'll get to that," Lee said. "But I have a story for you first. Nearly fifty years ago, in the kitchen right behind us, Alabama state troopers began clubbing a man on the floor. All he'd done was join some marchers who were going to stand in front of a jail and sing hymns for someone who had been arrested for helping to register black voters. State troopers busted up the march and chased people, including the man they trapped in the kitchen. Jimmie Lee Jackson, who tried to protect the man being clubbed."

Webb remembered the engraving on the memorial.

26 • FEB • 1965 JIMMIE LEE JACKSON • CIVIL RIGHTS MARCH • KILLED BY STATE TROOPER • MARION, AL

Lee stared at his coffee cup for a few moments. He lifted his left hand off the table and reached over with his thumb and forefinger to pluck and lift the loose skin on the back of his right hand.

"This," he said, "was the color of that man's skin. Same as mine. Black. Some folks want to call us African-American. I'm okay with that, but I prefer black. It's what I am. Black."

Lee looked Webb straight in the eyes. "Ever had people sitting in cars at an intersection lock their doors when they notice you on the sidewalk waiting for a light to change? Ever had store owners follow you up and down the aisles to make sure you don't steal something?"

Webb shook his head. When he'd been living on the streets, he'd worked hard to look groomed and clean. Otherwise, he supposed he would have faced the same thing.

"It's because you're white," Lee said. "Let me tell you, when that stuff happens, it feels like there's acid sitting in your stomach. It sits there for a long time after too."

Lee took a breath. "Almost fifty years ago, the black man in the kitchen getting clubbed by troopers? He was eighty-two years old. His daughter, Viola, tried to pull the troopers away, and they began beating her too. That's when the grandson stepped in and tried to help his mother and his grandfather. Grandson's name was Jimmie Lee Jackson. A state trooper shot him twice in the belly, and they beat him with clubs as he staggered out of this café. Jimmie Lee Jackson died about a week later in the hospital. Nurse there said she saw powder burns on his belly. Trooper was that close when he pulled the trigger, it left powder burns. Grand jury back then didn't feel there was enough evidence for the trooper to go to trial. A few years back, he finally did get charged with first-degree murder. He pled guilty to manslaughter and only got six months in jail. What a slap in the face of justice. I want you to give this a minute of silence, just to think about it."

One part of Webb wanted to protest. The injustice wasn't his fault.

But a bigger part of Webb could see it happening. The clubs coming down on an old man who had believed that singing hymns was a good way to make a statement. A man on the floor who looked up and saw troopers shoot his grandson in the belly, a grandson who had tried to protect him. Troopers. Men who were supposed to protect people and uphold the law.

Webb let out a deep sad breath. Only fifty years ago?

"Yesterday, much as you irritated me, I knew just enough about you and the efforts you'd made to help Ruby that I thought it would be worthwhile to spend a little time getting you to see things from my point of view," Lee said after the moment of silence had passed. "I needed those Camaro parts from Roy Hawkins anyway, and I thought the money I spent sending you to Montgomery would be a good investment if it taught you to look at the world through my eyes, if only for a minute or two. That's how change is made. One person at a time."

Lee lifted the skin on the back of his hand again, then let it drop. "Maybe you're thinking that it was a lot more time and effort than necessary to bring you right here to Marion. Jimmie Lee Jackson's death sparked a huge march, you know. It did make a difference eventually. But that's not why we are sitting here. First reason is, I needed to disappear. I'm using throwaway cell phones and cash only. This place was as good as any to meet you and stay on the run."

He caught the look that Webb was unable to hide.

"Yeah," Lee said. "I'm on the run. No doubt. Why? All I did was make a few phone calls about those identification cards."

Lee tapped the side of his coffee cup, as if he had too much nervous energy and didn't know what to do with it. "I was sixteen when all this happened here. This is my hometown. I could have been part of the hymn singing that night, but I thought it wasn't my business. I was wrong. Later, I marched from Selma to Montgomery, and I faced down troopers who wanted to shoot us in the crowd. What happened that night in the café—it changed me. You should know that about me, because it looks like we are going to be spending some time together. That's because you and I will be asking some questions in the next few days, and we won't be trusting a single one of the people we ask. You're going to be on the run with me. Unless you want out."

The waitress set down two orders of meatloaf. Webb looked across the steaming dishes at Lee.

"In," Webb said. "Want to tell me more about what happened last night?"

Webb began to pick at his food, mainly just moving it around on the plate.

"I heard the fire alarm coming from my garage," Lee said, also leaving his food untouched. "I looked out my window, and it was already in flames. I tried calling the fire department, but my landline was out. My cell phone wouldn't work either. I ran outside, thinking maybe I could do something with my garden hose, but all I could do was watch the garage burn. Motorcycle and Camaro inside. When I turned around, my house was on fire. Some people might think I was lucky, getting out of the house in time, but I don't. I'm guessing whoever set the garage on fire did it to get me out of the house. What they really wanted to do was burn down the house. Can you think of a reason why?"

Webb shook his head. A bite of meatloaf tasted like sawdust to him. He put ketchup on it.

"Two identification cards," Lee said. "Somebody with the ability to cut off my landline and jam my cell-phone signals wanted the cards destroyed so that nobody could prove they existed. Somebody who later listened in on my call to Roy Hawkins. That was my test. First thing in the morning, I called from my cell and told Roy he could find you at the Civil Rights Memorial later in the afternoon. That gave whoever it was all day to send someone there. The fact that someone showed up told me they were monitoring my calls. Two identification cards. They can't be worried about the names, because those are easy to memorize. It must be the photographs they want destroyed, so that no one can prove one soldier had two cards in two different names."

"Them?" Webb said. "Who is them? Gangsters from BTK?"

"Someone higher up, is my guess," Lee said. "Someone who could send BTK after you. Someone who found out I was asking about those cards and wanted the questions to stop. As I mentioned, someone with considerable resources. Let's just call him the Bogeyman."

"Bogeyman? I thought that was an imaginary monster."

"Imaginary until we track him down. Both cards burned in the house though. That's going to make it a lot tougher on us."

"I've still got both." Webb set his iPhone on the table. "I saved them in the cloud."

He pulled up the photos he'd taken of the identification cards. Jesse Lockewood. Benjamin Moody. Two names. One face.

Lee grinned.

"All right then," he said. "The two of us are in business. And it's time for payback. Let's track down the Bogeyman. First stop, Atlanta."

# NINE

From the restaurant, Lee and Webb walked half a block. Lee pulled out a key fob and clicked the button. Ahead of them, chirping sounds came from a gleaming black Camaro parked in front of a hardware store.

"I'll drive the first half of the trip," Lee said. "You drive the second. Like our ride?"

"Almost invisible," Webb said. "Nobody will notice us at all."

Lee laughed. "Had one of my employees rent it in his name. We're off the radar, unless we get pulled over for speeding. But Roy and I have a weakness for fast cars and motorcycles. I figure if we're going on a road trip, we're going to do it in style."

Lee opened the trunk. Webb saw a suitcase and a computer bag. Webb put his guitar travel bag in, shut the trunk and slipped into the passenger seat. Bucket seats. Leather. Tinted windows. It wasn't a bad ride.

As Lee put on his seat belt, Webb asked, "You and Roy are good friends, right?"

"He's a redneck and I'm a civil-rights activist. Couldn't find two people farther apart in ideology. But we fought back-to-back in jungles and in elephant grass. I know he'd die for me, and I'd die for him."

Lee turned on the ignition, and the Camaro rumbled. He eased it forward. As they moved beneath the streetlights, Webb said, "You called Roy and told him I'd be at the Civil Rights Memorial. Roy said you both wanted to see if anyone would show up to prove that someone was tapping your phone."

"Yup. Now we know we need to stay off the radar."

"If someone is looking for us, why wouldn't they have gone right to the junkyard when Ali first took me there? They know you and Roy are friends. That's where I was supposed to go anyway."

"Roy was hoping they would," Lee said. "Anybody inside the gates would have been trapped. And trespassing. Battle strategy. It would have given him a chance to find out who sent them. But it didn't work out that way, so that's why we're going on this road trip to Atlanta. I want a face-to-face with the person I called about those identification cards. We're going to go all the way up and down the chain of people who asked questions about them, and find out who was worried enough about those cards to burn down my property. My gut says government. But someone in the government who can't work in the open; otherwise they would have gone to Roy's junkyard. Which means this Bogeyman has something to hide, and once we find out what it is, we'll nail him. Or her. Or them."

They reached the outskirts of town, going north on Highway 5, and Lee eased the car up to the higher speed limit.

"We've got about four hours," Lee said. "There's an iPad in the backseat. Why don't you grab it?"

Webb reached around and set it on his lap.

"That's our KITT," Lee said.

"KITT?"

"From *Knight Rider*. A television series in the eighties. About a guy who fought bad guys with the help of a car that could talk to him—KITT. Science fiction then. But Siri will answer our questions, map out where we need to go, give advice on restaurants. Not quite like a car talking to us, but close enough. And we'll have entertainment too. I loaded a movie on it that I'd like you to watch while we drive. *Casablanca*."

"That's an old movie. Black-and-white?"

"Classic. Greatest film ever. You're stuck with me, and it'll give us something to talk about after you've seen it."

"Sure," Webb said. He began to pull up the movie on the device.

"Not so fast," Lee said. "I need some truth from you. Restaurant wasn't the place for it. I wanted you in a place where you couldn't run away when I asked."

It struck Webb then how completely he'd trusted a stranger. What did Webb know about Lee Knox? Maybe Lee had been lying about everything. And now Webb was stuck in a vehicle moving at sixty miles an hour on a dark highway somewhere in the middle of Alabama. All Lee had to do was pull out some kind of weapon...

"First," Lee said, "look at it from my point of view. Some kid shows up out of nowhere, hands me two pieces of military ID from the Vietnam War and wonders if I can ask some questions about them. I make a couple of phone calls and ask those questions, and within hours it's obvious that somebody is willing to risk ten years in a federal prison to burn down my house and destroy those cards. You with me so far?"

"So far," Webb said.

"So I need to know how you got those cards in the first place and why you wanted those questions asked. That's going to go a long ways toward helping us find the Bogeyman."

Webb hesitated before answering.

Lee caught the hesitation, and his voice came out of the darkness, his face glowing slightly in the light from the dashboard. "Here's the deal, son. If you don't want to answer, I'll respect that. Birmingham is up ahead, and I'll drop you off at a hotel near the bus station and pay for the room and give you enough money to get back to Nashville in the morning. Then Roy and I keep looking for answers without you, because this is personal now, and if you don't want any part of it, you can bail out of the fight.

But if you're in, you don't lie. I will take you on your word of honor about that. Take as much time as you need to make your choice. Birmingham's at least an hour down the road."

Headlights from an approaching car cut through the windshield. Webb saw that Lee's eyes were focused on the highway.

Webb said, "What's my guarantee that you'll keep me involved once I tell you everything? For all I know, you'll leave me behind somewhere and keep looking without me."

"You still have the photos of the identification cards in the cloud," Lee said. "I need those. Without you, I can't access them."

That was true. Webb decided it was enough protection for him. But he had another question.

"What I tell you stays between us?" Webb asked.

"Word of honor," Lee said. "As long as *us* includes Roy. Ali too. We're a team."

Webb made his decision. "It started in a cabin by a lake in Ontario. Five of us," he said.

# TEN

"Last year," Webb told Knox, "my grandfather David McLean died. I have six cousins, all guys, all about my age. In his will, he left each of us a task and the money it would take to complete the task. My cousin DJ went to Africa. Steve to Spain. Adam to France. Bunny and Spencer stayed in Canada. And Rennie went to Iceland. Me? Grandfather sent me to the Northwest Territories, and I hiked a remote trail. Led me to discover something that happened about sixty years ago."

"Ruby Gavin's father," Lee said. "The funeral in Eagleville."

"And more than that."

David McLean had hired a private investigator to dig up information on Webb's stepfather, information that had removed the stepfather as a threat from Webb's life and the life of his mother. Not Lee's business though.

Webb instead told Lee about the other legacy. "Grandfather left money for me to get some songs recorded in Nashville. I did that before Christmas, and then I went back to Canada for a visit."

Webb wondered if he should explain how the producer seemed to be ripping him off and how he was still trying to get back the copies of the songs. Webb decided against that too. It wasn't anyone's business but his own.

"The day after Christmas," Webb continued, "all the grandsons who were around decided to spend the day at our grandfather's cottage, in honor of his memory."

Webb could easily picture it. The snow-plowed driveway marked by an old, handmade mailbox in the shape of a beehive. The cottage that had begun as a few bedrooms and a stone fireplace in a central room, with more and more rooms added on over the years.

Webb had driven up to the cottage with Adam, happy to listen to him talk about movies. Webb wasn't about to talk about his troubles with a sleazy producer in Nashville.

"We were nearly out of firewood, and it was cold. Spencer was pulling at a log beside the fireplace and didn't know that it was actually nailed in place to hide a panel behind it. First thing that came out when the panel pulled loose was a Walther PPK."

"You Canadians even know what that is?" Lee said. "I thought the only weapons you had up there were snowballs."

"Ha, ha," Webb answered. "We watch movies too. A Walther PPK is what Bond uses. But trust me, we were rattled. What would our grandfather be doing with a hidden weapon?"

"Take your time with this," Lee said. "We've got more than two hundred miles ahead of us, and you've got my full interest."

"My cousin Bunny is a cool kid," Webb said. "Kind of lives in his own world. He got hold of the gun, and when he pulled the trigger—"

"Not loaded," Lee interrupted. "Tell me it wasn't loaded."

"Bunny didn't think so. It was very loud. Understatement. Nobody got hurt though. And that wasn't the most dangerous thing we found."

There'd been a mesh bag full of golf balls, but confusing as that was, it didn't seem relevant, so Webb described the money instead.

"My grandfather had hidden a bag full of money behind the panel," Webb said. "Lots of currencies. I mean, lots. Ten thousand in American. Ten thousand in Canadian. Five thousand British pounds, five thousand Euros. Argentinian pesos. Russian rubles. We wanted to believe it was there because he'd made a good living as an importer/exporter. That's what everyone had believed while he was alive."

"That makes sense," Lee said.

"But the passports didn't. British. Spanish. American. Russian. German. About a dozen. Each of them with his photo, and each of them with a different name."

"Import/export," Lee said. "You were thinking…"

"Yeah," Webb said. "Spy. It didn't help that there were some disguises in the bag too. It was hard to comprehend. Who had our grandfather been? Someone we never really knew like we thought we did? A spy?"

"Not necessarily," Lee said. "Maybe there was another explanation."

"Like what?" Webb asked.

They traveled about a mile in silence. Lee broke it first. "Okay, maybe there isn't another explanation. But if he was working for the Canadian government, that makes him a good guy. And, of course, he'd have to keep it hidden from his family. We have the CIA. You guys have…"

"CSIS. Canadian Security Intelligence Service."

"So he probably spent his life helping Canada then."

"Except…" Webb said. He needed to gather himself to continue. He'd promised Lee the truth and all of it. That didn't make it easy though.

"Except?"

"We found a small black notebook too." Webb could picture Adam holding it up after he'd found it in the back corner of the hidden cubbyhole. "There was a note from our grandfather in it."

Webb pulled out his iPhone. He'd taken a photo of the note, and now he read it to Lee.

"*I hoped I'd never have to use this book, but I needed to keep my own record, my own account, in case things ever came tumbling down around me. Maybe I know better than anybody that you can never trust anything or anyone, and I needed proof of who I was and what I did. I just know that I always did what needed to be done. Nothing more, and nothing less."*

"Good guy," Lee said. "Cautious. Wants to make sure there's no blowback."

"Blowback?"

"Repercussions. It's a gun expression for burns from exploding powder."

Webb sighed. It was a heavy load, only made easier because he knew his six cousins were bearing it with him. "The notebook was divided into sections. One for each passport. From when my grandfather was younger. A lot of it was written in what looked like code. There was also an envelope that fell out as we opened it. You could see the imprint of some words on the front. *You are a traitor. You deserve to die."*

"Nice Christmas present," Lee said.

"And a Happy New Year. Our parents didn't expect us back until New Year's Day, so some of us decided to take the week to do what we could to prove he wasn't a traitor. We're going to report back to each other at the end of the week. Adam, DJ and I each chose passports and the currency that went with them. DJ sent stuff to Steve in Spain, and Adam to Rennie in South America. Bunny couldn't leave the country, so he and his brother, Spencer took some other stuff."

"Long shot," Lee said. "Especially if your grandfather *was* involved with CSIS. Most things would be under wraps. Ancient history too."

"You'd think," Webb said. "Except here we are, on a highway at night, because someone burned your house and garage to the ground. Maybe not so ancient history."

They both gave that some thought. Then Lee said, "Your grandfather had an American passport? That's why you're here?"

"It's the fake Canadian passport I'm worried about. With his photo and in the name Sean Alexander. It had stamps from entry into Saigon and Paris. The dates were in the seventies. Both the identification cards I left with you were in the passport, tucked between the pages. I only found them after I left the cottage."

"Easy conclusion that it has something to do with the Vietnam War." Lee grunted. "I was talking to

Roy on the phone while Ali was giving you a ride to Marion. He says the guy who tried to take you at the memorial was a Vietnamese gangster."

"Maybe this helps," Webb said. After telling this much, there was no point holding back the rest. "The Sean Alexander passport also had two other identification cards tucked between the pages. Not military, just ID. One for a man and one for a woman. Both Vietnamese."

"Yeah," Lee said. "It does help. All of it points to Vietnam and the war. If we can find out what the link is, we'll get our answers. If your grandfather was a spy, you want to prove he wasn't a traitor. Me? I want payback for a burned-down house."

# ELEVEN

The next morning at seven, Webb was sitting in a booth at a breakfast restaurant across the street from the Atlanta motel where Lee had paid for two rooms the night before.

This was a new day. Webb had changed from his Blue Bombers T-shirt to his Calgary Stampeders. Iconic white galloping horse against a red background. Six for thirteen in Grey Cup appearances. If you wanted to see a beautiful city, you had to check out Calgary. Rocky Mountains for a backdrop, wide open plains spread out in front. Home of Canada's Sports Hall of Fame.

Webb held his iPhone at arm's length and smiled and took a selfie. His mom knew that he was in the States, just not all the things he was doing.

"There's proof of a generation that thinks it's important," Lee said. "The world revolves around you guys, right?"

"Or proof that every morning I email a new photo to my mom," Webb said. "Subject heading, Smile of the Day. That way she knows I'm thinking about her and that I love her."

"Don't I feel like a pompous ass," Lee said. "Give your mom my best."

Webb bent over his phone to compose the email and attach the new photo. It would be the usual email, telling her that everything was great and that he missed her. No sense making her worry when she was so far away. That's when someone slid a pile of twenty-dollar bills onto the table and sat down at their booth.

The man was in paint-splattered jeans and an old work shirt. Webb had seen him pull up in an old pickup with a sign on its door: *JOHNSON RENOVATING.*

"Don't want the money from you," the man said to Lee. "Be nice if you answered some questions, but if you don't, I'm fine with that too. I'll tell you what you want either way. That Purple Heart of yours gives you as much credit as you need with me."

Lee left the money where it was. "I'm taking you away from work. You should be compensated for it."

The man's name was Marcus Johnson, and he was a few years younger than Lee. He had a goatee, and his nose looked like it had been flattened by punches a few times. His skin was ebony black, and the wrinkles around his eyes showed that he laughed plenty.

"I'll just get to the job site late and stay a little later," Marcus said. "You're not paying me to help, and I hope I've made that clear."

The waitress stopped at the table. She was mid-twenties. Her hair was in cornrows. She held a pencil and a pad, and her fingernails were clipped short. No rings. Normally, Webb didn't give much thought to skin color, but it occurred to him that he was the only white person in the restaurant. White. He decided he preferred that to calling himself Caucasian. Put him in Lee's camp when it came to color definitions, although it'd be nice to live in a world where all that mattered was the shared color of blood.

"You have kids?" Lee asked the waitress. Friendly.

She put a hand on her hip, cocked her head and said, "What kind of way is that to order breakfast?"

"Two eggs over easy, pancakes, bacon," Lee said. "You have kids? Humor me."

She wrote the order down, looked up and said, "Two boys. Five and three. Best thing that happened to me. Any other questions?"

Lee shook his head. "Nope."

Webb ordered the same thing as Lee. Marcus chose an omelet.

"Notice her fingernails?" Lee asked Marcus.

Marcus shrugged.

"Webb?" Lee said.

"Clipped short," Webb answered.

"That's what I saw too," Lee said. "She's working hard, doesn't spend money on fingernails. Some places I go, women have long curving nails with artwork on glossy paint. Takes money to maintain. Nails that long and beautiful, you make sure they don't get chipped, means you're more worried about your nails than doing a good job. I see nails like hers, cut short, tells me that for her, it's all about take-home pay for her two boys. That sound about right?"

"I'd rather hear about where you're going and why I'm here," Marcus said. "Some girl on a motorcycle stops by my house last night and hands me an envelope with money, as a thank-you for my time, and instructions to show up here at 7 AM and make sure nobody follows me. I'm more curious about that than what somebody does with their fingernails."

Lee straightened out the twenties, but left them on the table. "If you don't take this cash, we should leave it as a tip for her, knowing it's probably going to be used for her two little boys and not for painted fingernails. That way, we both get to feel good about helping her and I won't feel like I put you in harm's way without making it worth your while."

"Harm's way?" Marcus asked.

"You got a call from Michael Durant, right?"

"Right."

"I'm trying to establish the chain of people who were involved in the questions I asked. He's a friend from way back to my time in 'Nam. I asked him if he had any connections to help me get information.

He named you. That makes you second in the chain. I'd like to know the next link after you."

"Makes me a friend of a friend, is what you're saying."

"Yeah. Durant told me he called you, wondering if you had any way of looking into the military background of two soldiers. Jesse Lockewood. Benjamin Moody. Durant was going to get back to me with what he learned from you, but stuff, um, happened."

"Yeah," Marcus answered. "He was up-front about it—said it was a favor to you. Said you were a stand-up guy and did three years in 'Nam. Purple Heart. That was good enough for me. I told him I could ask someone I knew still in the military, and I did."

"The person you asked. The next link in the chain. You give him my name?"

"I did. Saw no reason not to mention it. Michael Durant didn't make like it was secret. What's that got to do with making sure no one followed me here and putting me in harm's way?"

"Someone burned down my house to get rid of the old identification cards."

Marcus turned his head and stared out the restaurant window. Gray sky, a few drops of rain. Not much to see except rundown storefronts. And the cheap motel where Webb and Lee had stayed the night before. But it didn't appear that Marcus was looking out the window for the view. He was thinking things through.

"Some reason then," Marcus finally said, "that those names are dangerous. Flagged in a military computer maybe?"

"Maybe," Lee said. "By someone with enough juice to shut down my cell signals and tap my cell phone."

"You got a burner cell now?" Marcus asked.

"Walmart special," Lee said. "Doesn't mean that they can't tap *your* incoming calls. If they knew you were somewhere along the chain, they could be watching you, waiting for me and the kid here."

Marcus gave a slow nod. "That's why I got a message on a piece of paper from you instead of a call."

"If you followed my instructions, you made sure no one followed you," Lee said. "We're both safe. Off-grid."

"Fair enough," Marcus said. "Thanks for covering me. Durant was right about you being a stand-up guy."

Marcus gave Webb some attention for the first time since sitting down. "How you involved?"

"I'm the one who started it all," Webb answered. "I asked Lee if he could help me."

"That's how I'd like it to stay," Lee said to Marcus. "You're helping me. Not Webb here."

"Message received loud and clear," Marcus said. "I'm in front of you now. What questions you have?"

"Same ones that Michael Durant had for you first time around. Except for a different reason. If I know your contact, maybe I can track down who wanted my house burned. Also, it would help if you gave me any information on the two names. Lockewood and Moody."

"First answer. I called General Sutton. I knew him long before he was an Air Force general. He told me he had to make a call to DC, to his contact there."

As in Washington, DC, Webb guessed.

"You have the name of the DC contact?" Lee asked.

"I can get it from Sutton and pass it along to you as soon as I find out."

"Thanks," Lee said. "Second answer?"

Marcus nodded. "Jesse Lockewood, 198th Infantry Delta Company Second Platoon. Shipped home in a body bag in '72. Was nineteen at the time.

Posthumous Bronze Star. Died in enemy fire while trying to evacuate three wounded. Saved the life of a solider named Casey Gardner."

"Parents still alive?"

"Mother gone. Father lives in Gainesville, Florida. Matt Lockewood. In his early eighties. Jesse's sister is Natasha Bartlett, lives in a place called Sandpoint, Idaho."

"Anything on Casey Gardner?" Lee asked. "Might be helpful to talk to him."

"He's officially listed as a deserter. No official trace of him since Vietnam."

"And Benjamin Moody?" Lee said.

"Here's what's strange," Marcus said. "He's got a full military record right up to his time in Vietnam. He served until '72, but after that, he disappears from any computer records. No record of tax returns, no driver's license, no social security contributions. No death certificate. It's like the guy completely vanished."

Lee tapped his spoon on the table as he gave it some thought. Then he asked, "You had a chance to tell any of this to my buddy Michael?"

"Nope. Just got it last night."

"How about calling him later this morning and giving him all the information?" Lee said. "Make sure it sounds like neither of us has any idea what's going on. If your phone is tapped, that might give me a leg up, because they'll have no idea that I've already learned all this."

"Done."

"Thanks," Lee said.

Lee slapped the table with a palm and stood and looked at Webb.

"Well," Lee said to him, "let's head back to Tennessee."

Webb looked back as they were leaving the restaurant. He saw the waitress fan the twenties in joy and disbelief as she stopped at the table to pick up her tip. Lee caught the look too, and gave her a thumbs-up so she'd know it wasn't a mistake.

Short fingernails. That did say something, didn't it?

# TWELVE

"What did you think of *Casablanca*?" Lee asked an hour into the road trip. "You know, the movie."

Lee sipped a coffee while Webb drove the Camaro, cruise control set at two miles per hour above the speed limit. They were on Interstate 75 heading south and had just passed a sign that said *Macon 10*. The Georgia countryside in December looked good to Webb, greener than in Nashville, five hours north, and plenty green compared to the gray city snow of Toronto. Webb loved the feel of the Camaro on the road and wished he could drive about twenty miles an hour faster.

"What did you think of *Casablanca*?" Lee repeated with no trace of impatience that Webb had ignored his question the first time.

The night before, alone in his motel room, Webb had watched *Casablanca* again on Lee's iPad before falling asleep. The actor Humphrey Bogart played the proprietor of a nightclub in Casablanca, a city in Morocco, on the African coast. Bogart got priceless letters of transit that would let refugees escape German control. Bogart sacrificed those letters to help the woman he loved leave with another man. Webb liked the line that Bogart said when he first saw her: "Of all the gin joints in all the towns in all the world, she walks into mine."

"*Casablanca*?" Webb said. "Before I tell you what I think, maybe you should be more up-front with me. You told the guy in the restaurant we were headed back to Nashville to visit your buddy. That's north. I'm nearly out of patience waiting for you to tell us why we're heading south."

"Nice to see you're paying attention."

"No answer?"

"I told him we were headed to Nashville in case he was reporting back to our Bogeyman. That gives us extra time before they find us."

"So where *are* we going?" Webb asked. "Maybe you haven't noticed, but there are two of us in this car."

"Gainesville, to visit Jesse Lockewood's father. Might as well see what we can learn from him. Who knows, maybe that's not even his son's photo on the ID card. While you were putting gas in the car, I called Roy Hawkins. He texted me Lockewood's address a few minutes ago."

"Nice of you to keep me informed," Webb said. "Like I did for you when you wanted full disclosure about the identification cards and my grandfather."

"Trust is something I don't do easily," Lee said. "I'd apologize, but it would be insincere."

"So that's how it is. I answer your questions, but you play Mr. Clam for me?"

"All I asked was if you liked *Casablanca*."

"Without telling me why you wanted me to watch it. Seems like somehow I've become your pet project, but this whole Grasshopper thing is old. Maybe you should tell me why you wanted me to watch it."

"Grasshopper?"

"Yeah. Like in the old Kung Fu movies. Where the master says something like, 'Grasshopper, when you can snatch the pebble from my hand, it is time for you to leave.' Thing is, and I say this with respect, I didn't sign up to be your student."

"What happened in Macon, Georgia," Lee said, "a few years before the Vietnam War?"

"Let me see," Webb answered. He wasn't sleeping much these days, and that made him irritable too. "I'll bet that somewhere, at some time, the traffic lights turned from green to yellow to red. Cars stopped. The lights turned green, and cars moved forward again. I'll bet that happened. Rain probably fell. Dogs pooped in parks. Babies dropped ice-cream cones on sidewalks. I could come up with a whole list of things that must have happened there before the war. Oops, that was me ignoring the pebble in your open hand."

Lee remained calm. "Early sixties, a black man named Billy Randall organized a boycott of the buses," Lee said. "Until then, blacks couldn't sit in a white section of a bus. So not one black took a bus for three weeks. Boycott ended three weeks later. No violence. No more segregation. Something we can learn from."

"I'm not your grasshopper."

"You're the next generation. Twenty, thirty years from now, you and your friends are going to be making the decisions that matter. Coal-fired generators for electricity? Or nuclear? Or solar-powered? Equality? No equality?"

"I don't think you're listening," Webb said. "You could have picked anyplace in Atlanta to meet that guy, but you took us to a restaurant in a part of town where people stare at me because my skin is white. Think I can't figure out you're trying to make a point about what it's like for a black man to be surrounded by whites? Let me repeat. I didn't sign up to be your grasshopper."

"And I didn't sign up to get my house burned down."

"Wondered when you'd bring that up," Webb said. "Wondered when you'd use it to make me feel guilty and do it your way."

Webb hit the signal light to indicate he was taking the next exit. He brought the Camaro to a stop on the shoulder at a safe place and gave Lee a cold smile.

"This long hair you think is the whole hip-musician look?" Webb said as he put the Camaro into Park. "Not that at all. I had a stepfather in the military who controlled every aspect of my life. Didn't *try* to control it. Controlled it. Right down to the buzz cut and signing me up for cadets. It's why I ran away from home and lived on the streets, eating from Dumpsters. I grew my hair out so that anytime he saw me after that, he'd see the hair that told him I was doing it my way, not his. And one of the ways he controlled me was just like you did. Guilt."

Webb unbuckled his seat belt. "Mr. Knox, thanks for all you've tried to do to help, but I'll be going my own way, if you don't mind."

Webb hit the button that popped the trunk. He stepped out of the car, took his guitar travel bag from the open trunk, slammed it shut and began walking up the hill that led to the overpass ahead. The weight of the guitar in the travel bag felt comforting to him. His guitar had never let him down.

Lee stepped out from the passenger side. "I'm sorry," he said. "Just listen, okay?"

Webb kept walking. Lee had to walk with him. A breeze blew from behind them, fanning the long grass in the ditch.

"No more guilt," Lee said. "Not your fault my house is gone. And trust me, it was well insured."

Lee stayed at Webb's side, keeping up. "My bad for pushing my agenda on you. I can't help it.

Two reasons. First, I've spent my whole life fighting for civil rights. It's who I am. It's wrong to be prejudiced against someone for the color of their skin. Second, it's not too difficult to see there's something good about you. You're better than drugs and rock and roll. Kids like you can make a difference, if you care."

"Now you accuse me of doing drugs? That's what the long hair says to you? Talk about prejudice. Maybe I need to make you my project."

"Come on," Lee said. "Look at me. From age ten, I've never asked a white person for any kind of help. I'm asking now. Don't walk away. Because you were right. I'm wrong to be forcing this on you."

"If I was black, you'd ask for help, no problem," Webb said. "That it? So you think it's wrong for a white person to be prejudiced against a black man for the color of his skin, but it's okay for a black man to be prejudiced against a white man for the same reason?"

"There's no doubt I'm an angry black man," Lee said. "In general, I've got good reason for it, but you're not interested in why, and I'll try to leave it be. In specific, right now I'm an angry black man because someone burned my house down. And I'm also angry at myself because you're a good kid and I could have found a better way to get you to see the world from my point of view. I'm asking forgiveness. You got that in you?"

Webb took a deep breath. The man beside him was proud; asking this could not have been easy.

"I got it in me," Webb said. "As long as you don't tell me to watch any more old movies."

Lee grinned. Like he understood Webb was trying to break the tension.

Lee said, "Won't tell you to do anything again. But I'll ask. Would you please watch just one more? And if you do, I'll buy you a steak dinner—biggest, most expensive steak you want. Tonight. After we talk to Jesse Lockwood's father in Gainesville."

Webb let out a long sigh and turned back to the Camaro.

"Lobster," Webb said over his shoulder to Lee. "Going to cost you a lobster on top of that steak."

"Then I drive the next shift and you take the iPad." Lee grinned. "The movie is *Ocean's Eleven*. The original from 1960. Starring Frank Sinatra. You have heard of Sinatra, haven't you, Grasshopper?"

Webb could have gotten mad again, but he knew Lee was teasing, and it didn't feel bad.

"Keep your pebble," Webb said. He hoped he'd have an appetite by evening. "I'm only in this for steak and lobster."

# THIRTEEN

Lee stopped the Camaro at a corner that led to a cul-de-sac in an old neighborhood in Gainesville. They'd made it from the rolling hills of Atlanta to the Florida state line in about three and a half hours, and the last ninety miles south from the state line had been all scrub bush and swamps and palmettos, the interstate jammed with semis and motorhomes.

In this subdivision, the pavement was cracked and patched with tar, and the houses were bungalows with faded stucco, dwarfed by the palmettos in the yards.

As Lee shut down the engine, Webb looked up from the iPad.

"You were buried in that thing," Lee said. "What did you do, watch the movie twice?"

"Didn't enjoy Sinatra quite as much as Bogart," Webb said, "so the answer is no. Last hour, I've been hitting Facebook. Hope you have a good data plan."

"Borrowed that iPad from one of the women who works for me," Lee said. "If I used my own device and my own data plan, chances are we could be tracked. Facebook?"

Webb tapped the iPad. "I think I found him."

"Him?"

"Matt Lockewood," Webb told Lee.

Webb tilted the iPad toward Lee and showed him the photos on the Facebook account.

"Facebook?" Lee said. "He's a bit old for that, wouldn't you say?"

"For a guy who doesn't like getting judged by appearances, you're quick to—"

"Yeah, yeah," Lee said. "Get over it."

"I might have to," Webb said. "I wasn't talking about his account. I think I found his daughter's account. Natasha Bartlett in Sandpoint, Idaho. Small town. Don't think it would have two Natasha Bartletts. Especially two with a father named Matt Lockewood."

Lee pulled the keys out of the ignition. "We'll see if the photo matches the man we're about to see."

"I take it we're in front of his house," Webb said.

"He's around the corner," Lee said. "I don't want him to know what vehicle we drove. Thought before we knocked on Lockewood's door, I'd give you a heads-up on our planned approach. You know, so you won't feel like the grasshopper here." Lee spread his hands, palms upward, like a magician trying to convince his audience that nothing was up his sleeves. "The new transparency. Like it?"

"Convenient transparency," Webb answered. "I notice that you pick and choose. If it was total transparency, you would have mentioned that Roy Hawkins has been following us since the last time we stopped for gas. He's—what, a block behind us? In a green Chevy half-ton, parked behind the moving van on the right-hand side of the street? Ali on the passenger side? Motorcycle strapped in place in the back of the truck?"

Lee stared at Webb, and then a huge grin crossed his face. "Not bad, son. You do pay attention."

Webb didn't know if he liked the fact that he enjoyed getting compliments from Lee. Webb didn't want to get into the habit of trying to earn the older man's approval.

"He's our backup," Webb said. Not a question.

A big black bug flew into the windshield of their motionless vehicle, bounced away and kept flying. Webb thought that's what life was all about. When things hit you out of nowhere, you pick yourself up and do your best to pretend nothing happened. Nobody's business how you felt.

"Yes, he's our backup," Lee said. "When the BTK guy showed up at the Civil Rights Memorial, that told us the Bogeyman was tapping my cell conversations. When Ali scooped you out of there, it told the Bogeyman that I was expecting him to tap my cell. When they didn't go to Roy's junkyard, it told me and Roy that the Bogeyman didn't need to take the chance there because he had other ways to track us that were less dangerous."

"He figured out ahead of time that the junkyard was a trap."

"Which tells us something else," Lee said. "The Bogeyman has good intel. He'd been able to dig deep enough into Roy's military records to know you don't want to mess with him. Man, if we'd been able to close those junkyard gates on the Bogeyman, let me tell you, by the time Roy was finished, we'd have learned everything we needed to know. Unless the Bogeyman was legit and called in some major firepower. But if the Bogeyman was legit, he would have just walked in and badged us."

"So since nobody has badged us yet, the Bogeyman is someone with good intel, who can't work in the open."

"Exactly," Lee said. "That works in our favor. Sooner or later, he's going to show up, or send someone to show up, not knowing Roy is behind us, ready to rock and roll and do some old-fashioned head thumping."

An image flashed into Webb's mind of massive Roy Hawkins holding some guy by the neck, the guy clawing uselessly at Roy's biceps as the guy's air supply diminished. Then Webb pictured himself in Roy's grip, because Roy had decided he didn't like the way Webb had held on to Ali through some of the turns on the motorcycle. Not so good.

Lee opened the car door and the smell of citrus hit Webb. "How about we walk from here?"

Webb stepped out on his side and stretched.

Not even the end of December, and the air was gloriously warm. Maybe summer would be too hot in Gainesville, but Webb could handle a few weeks here now. Sit on a front porch, listen to the crickets, play his guitar.

No, wait—that wouldn't work. He was dodging someone with the power to tap phones and the motivation to burn houses. All because his grandfather might have been a spy or, worse, a traitor. That thought messed with his enjoyment of the weather and the outline of palmetto leaves etched against blue sky.

"What I'm hoping," Lee said as they walked around the corner, "is that Marcus was up front with us in Atlanta and that the Bogeyman has zero idea we even know about Jesse Lockewood's father. I'd rather see if Matt Lockewood can tell us anything now and save Roy's ability to head-thump for later, when we know more about the situation."

"We just knock on the door?" Webb asked.

"Better than calling ahead," Lee said. "Don't want to give warning. It would be smart to work on the assumption that the Bogeyman tapped Matt Lockewood's phone to cover all bases, guessing that sooner or later we'd learn about him. It's why we have to make all our visits in person. We have to assume the Bogeyman can tap into any phone, anytime."

"Dingdong," Webb said. "*Hello, sir. Interested in buying some cookies? And by the way, I hear your son Jesse died in Vietnam. Can you tell us why his photo is on two different identification cards?*"

"Grasshopper," Lee said. "You forget who I am."

"Angry black man," Webb answered. "Longtime civil-rights activist."

"Also a successful insurance broker. How about dingdong, *here's my business card, I'm from State Farm. Mind if I ask you a few questions about your son Jesse?* That buys us time inside the house to look for photos on the walls. Anything we learn from questions is a bonus."

"Dishonest," Webb said. "Hoping he'll assume the insurance thing is related to his son and maybe he's got some money coming for an old policy."

"And burning down a house isn't dishonest?"

Maybe later, Webb would tell Lee about the lesson Webb learned when he went to the North. That if you attack a monster the same way the monster attacks you, the danger is that you will become like the monster.

Webb said, "I'd prefer to be up front, tell him that I'm from Canada and that my grandfather might have known his son and would it be okay to ask a few questions. That should work. All across the world, people love Canadians."

"Someone of his generation sees me, and I don't show him a business card and let him see I'm a respectable businessperson," Lee said, "chances are he's going to think I'm there to rob his house. We won't get past the doorstep."

"You are racist," Webb said. "Not all whites are like that. Besides, people love Canadians. After I introduce myself, maybe he'll think you're an African-Canadian instead of an African-American. It'll all be good."

"Very funny, you are." Lee shrugged as they stopped in front of the final house on the street. "Try it your way then."

The house had been painted pink a long time ago. The stucco was cracked. The lawn was patchy. There was a weathered hammock hanging from supports on the front porch.

They walked to the front door.

Webb rang the bell.

They heard footsteps. A stooped man who had once been tall answered the door and only opened it halfway, still wearing a housecoat although it was past noon. He had a couple days' worth of gray stubble on a face that was an unhealthy gray. He didn't quite look like his Facebook photo but close enough.

"Hello, Mr. Lockewood," Webb said.

Matt Lockewood looked past Webb and glared with suspicion at Lee. He pushed the door partially closed, leaving just enough space to peer at them, and spoke with a chill in his voice. "Not interested."

"My name is Jim Webb," Webb said.

"You need a haircut," Matt told him. "How did you know my name?"

"Facebook," Webb said.

"Farcebook," Matt spat. "Bad enough families get together for Thanksgiving. Then my daughter sets up an account for me and expects me to put stuff on it. Yeah, today I had a big bowel movement. Should post that for the world."

"I'm from Canada," Webb said, feeling an ache from holding a fake smile in place. "I think my grandfather knew your son, Jesse. Would it be okay if I asked you some questions about him?"

Matt shut the door on Webb and Lee. As Webb took that opportunity to notice the fissures in the dry wood of the door and the varnish that flaked from it like yellowing cellophane, Matt's muffled voice came through the door.

"You've got thirty seconds to get off my property," Matt said, "or I call the cops. And I'm starting the count now. Thirty. Twenty-nine. Twenty-eight…"

Webb and Lee were out of earshot by the time the countdown reached fifteen.

As they moved past the gate and onto the street, Lee turned to Webb. "Tell me that part again, how all across the world, people love Canadians."

# FOURTEEN

Lee's iPad pinged. He was on the passenger side, working Google as Webb drove. They were on Highway 301, heading north to Jacksonville. Webb liked all the moving. Different landscapes, different towns. The hum of highway, flashing of power poles on the side of the car.

And silence.

Lee didn't need to listen to the radio or a CD, and he didn't talk unless something needed discussing. Webb was fine with that. It didn't hurt that he was driving a black Camaro with tinted windows. Except for the gnawing worry about his grandfather's past, Webb loved the sense of adventure that came with moving, moving, moving. Maybe that was something he had to learn about himself, that he wasn't going to be the kind of guy who wanted a nine-to-five job and a house with a picket fence. His grandfather hadn't wanted that either. His grandfather had always been...moving. This shared restlessness gave Webb a sudden new appreciation for his grandfather.

For a second, he didn't realize Lee had been talking to him, and Webb swam upward from his deep pool of thought and broke surface, returning to the moment.

"Next stop, Derek Irvine," Lee said. "Lives in Charleston. How's your American geography?"

"Saskatoon, Saskatchewan," Webb said, hiding in a grin.

"What kind of foreign language is that?" Lee asked, not joking. "Or did you just sneeze?"

"Name of a city and province in Canada," Webb said. "If you're going to test me on American geography, I'll do the same for you. What's the name of our president?"

"Nice try. Prime minister."

"Points to you," Webb answered. "Charleston. South Carolina, right? Civil War started there."

"Good job. Fort Sumter. Cannon fired there started it all. But freeing the slaves wasn't enough. A hundred years later—" Lee stopped himself. "Sorry, Grasshopper."

"Look," Webb said, "now that you're giving me a choice, I'm cool talking about what matters to you. Just not cool about watching Sinatra again. I don't get why people liked him in movies."

"Dang," Lee said. "I knew there was a reason I was beginning to like you."

"Those movies were a test?"

"Yup," Lee said.

Webb waited for more of an explanation, but it didn't come. Instead, Lee tapped his phone.

"We're headed to DC," Lee said. "From here, it's maybe eleven hours up Interstate 95."

Webb nodded. They were going to DC to visit the next person up the chain with information on Jesse Lockewood and Benjamin Moody, hoping it would lead them to the Bogeyman who'd burned down Lee's house.

Lee continued, "I've been googling Lockewood's platoon, trying to locate a soldier in his squad."

Again, Webb nodded. Lee had explained that there were four platoons to a company, thirty-six soldiers to a platoon and three twelve-soldier squads per platoon. That broke down further to three four-soldier fire teams. Lee and Roy had been on the same fire team.

"Found two of them," Lee said. "One in Wyoming, one in Charleston, South Carolina. Going to Wyoming takes us thirty-six hours west, and then another thirty-six hours east to DC. Or if you want, we can head for Charleston and Derek Irvine, which is only a small detour off Interstate 95 on the way north."

"Wow. Another seventy-two hours in a car with you if we chose Wyoming?"

"Not that you're the princess of fun," Lee said. He set the iPad in his lap and leaned back in the passenger seat. He rested his hands behind his head and stretched out his elbows, the picture of a man satisfied with a job well done. "My travel app shows we should get to Charleston about 6 PM. Hopefully, we can see Lockewood's squad mate tonight."

Webb said, "Before or after the steak and lobster you owe me?"

"Your choice," Lee said. He was looking at the iPad. "What the—?"

"What the what?"

"The Facebook account for Matt Lockewood's daughter? It's disappeared."

The Bogeyman, Webb thought, is everywhere. And he didn't feel like making a joke about it.

# FIFTEEN

"Let's talk about long hair," Lee said.

"How about not?" Webb answered. "Sixty miles left to Charleston. I want to enjoy the scenery."

It consisted of thick stands of pine trees on each side of the interstate. And billboards. Not spectacular. But better than talking about Webb's hair.

"I want to apologize," Lee said. "It bothers me that when I met you I called you a long-haired punk. Maybe you tell me more about why you like it long, and I'll tell you why I can't help but react when I see it long on a kid."

"Apology accepted," Webb said. "Time for me to enjoy the scenery."

"No other way to say this, but when I see long hair today, I see a kid trying to be cool."

"Look at those pine trees," Webb said. "Oh boy."

"When I was in 'Nam, kids your age were protesting the same war I didn't believe in fighting. They were part of a generation questioning all the values of the generation before them. Grew their hair long out of rebellion. At least they had the guts and passion to protest in peaceful groups. I wish kids today cared about something more than sitting in front of a television or a video game. At Kent State, National Guard shot into a crowd of antiwar protesters. Killed a few of them. Can you believe that happened in this country?"

"It's a good thing," Webb said, finally allowing himself to be drawn into the conversation, "that it's so hard to believe."

"Good thing?"

"Be a bad thing if it wasn't shocking. Like when I found out about those Sunday-school girls getting killed by a bomb in a church in Alabama. So wrong, it's hard to imagine. But stuff like that is happening in Iraq every day, and you get numb to it. There. Not here."

"But there's still lots to do," Lee said. "Discrimination has shifted from not allowing black people to sit in the same restaurant to black people earning less than white people, getting fewer jobs than white people, going to jail more than white people. That's what makes me angry."

"You want me to be angry about it too? Maybe I'll just go back to enjoying the view of pine trees."

"I'll be angry if you don't get angry. I want more people thinking about it. Black people and white people. More people thinking about it means maybe more people trying to do something about it. When I was your age, musicians came up with songs about fighting injustice and creating peace for the world. Now I turn on the radio, I hear songs that glorify taking drugs and getting somewhere alone with a girl. We don't need any more teenage mothers having babies with no fathers around to help raise them. Guy like you, maybe you could come up with another song like 'One Tin Soldier.' Make a difference, not just make money. Be like Bogart. Not Sinatra."

Webb might have resented getting a lecture like this from Lee, but it wasn't just a lecture. There was passion in it. And Webb couldn't help his curiosity.

"Not Sinatra?"

"Each of them, for a time, the biggest names in Hollywood. Bogart, he was cynical. You saw that in *Casablanca*."

"His character was cynical. Not Bogart. Rick was cynical. Bogart just played Rick's role."

"An actor like Bogart," Lee said, "who can take any role he wants, is only going to take a role he likes, is going to want to become the hero he portrays. You with me there?"

Webb didn't disagree, and Lee continued.

"In the end of *Casablanca*, you see Bogart making a sacrifice. To me, Bogart was cynical and tired of the world, but he believed in old-fashioned truth and justice. Was willing to die for his beliefs. I knew soldiers in 'Nam, they hated being there, hated the war, but they were serving a bigger cause. We were cynical about the war and plenty tired of it, but until our country told us to stop serving, we were going to do our duty and do what it took to protect the men on each side of us. The biggest compliment I can give Roy Hawkins? He's Bogart in *Casablanca*. Smart. Square but smart, and doesn't care if people think he's square, because he's going to do the right thing. But we had guys in our platoon, they wanted to be Sinatra. *Hate* is a strong word, but he was an actor I hated."

Webb couldn't recall having a conversation like this with his stepfather. Webb's father had died when Webb was young, but he liked to think they might have talked like this.

"Sinatra?" Webb said, to let Lee know he had dropped his attitude and was listening. It was better talking about Sinatra than trying to dodge a discussion about long hair.

"Sinatra came along and replaced Bogart," Lee said. "Sinatra represented hip. Hip is a fake type of cool. You try to wear it like a hat or a coat. Hip said that values were for losers. Hip didn't get into fights that cool might lose. Hip got other people to fight those fights. Great reporter named Mike Kelley said something like that. Same reporter who died covering the invasion of Iraq in 2003, when he could have been safe back in the States. Hip was all about taking care of yourself and looking good while you did it. Kent State, those kids that got killed protesting the war I was fighting? What we shared was a belief that values mattered, even if we disagreed about those values. Took me a while to understand that, and believe me, I didn't understand it when I first got back to the States from my tour and people spat on my uniform as I walked through the airports. But at least they cared enough to protest. Cared enough to spit. Never did like those long-hairs, but I couldn't help but respect that they believed in something."

Webb said, "So hip doesn't spit. Hip doesn't protest."

"Hip doesn't spit," Lee said. "Hip doesn't protest. Hip doesn't get involved. What I'm seeing now is kids posting photos of themselves on Facebook accounts that're all about them, and kids bullying other kids who are different and not trying to be cool. What I'm seeing now is an entire generation of kids who want to be Sinatra. Not Bogart. Today, kids have long hair, it's just to be cool. At least back then they did it because they believed in something."

Webb waited for more, but that was all Lee said, as if he wanted it to sink in while they covered the miles and miles of interstate in their quiet little world.

Webb reached for his iPhone.

"See?" Lee said. "Perfect example. We've got something here worth discussing, and you're looking to escape in your device."

"No," Webb said. "Going to download a song and listen to it. Give me a minute here."

It took less than a minute to get it on his phone. Another thirty seconds to connect to the car sound system by Bluetooth.

Lee said nothing, giving Webb the time he'd requested.

Webb played the opening notes, then paused the song.

"Flute and snare drum leading into violins?" Webb said to Lee. "Kind of…"

"Kind of seventies," Lee said. "But that only matters if you're worried about whether it's a cool enough song for you."

"Nice jab," Webb said. He'd been thinking it was kind of cheesy, not kind of "seventies." But he didn't say that, because it was obvious Lee liked the song enough to hold it up as an example of music that mattered.

Webb tapped the Play button and the song continued. *Listen, children to a story / that was written long ago / 'bout a kingdom on the mountain / and the valley folk below.*

Webb fought the impulse to make another critical statement, but it would only prove Lee's point.

Nothing about the beginning of the lyrics was cool.

The song continued until the title finally made sense, coming from the chorus.

*There won't be any trumpets blowing / come the judgment day / On the bloody morning after / one tin soldier rides away.*

When the song finished, Webb said to Lee, "You're right—not a Sinatra song. Mind if I play it again?"

The tune of the song wasn't really relevant, Webb thought. Part of what made it cheesy was that it was set in a major key. Approaching it from a minor key would give it a moody, dark feel instead of a sing-along-around-the-campfire feel.

But the message…that was something different. It made Webb want to get back to his music dreams, if only just for a single song.

Maybe when he got back to Nashville, he would find a studio and recut the song. Get rid of the flute and trumpets and violin and make it something Bogart would listen to.

*One tin soldier rides away.*

# SIXTEEN

They found Derek Irvine in an antique shop on Broad Street in the heart of the old part of Charleston, but not until Lee had first spent half an hour cruising the mansions that overlooked the waters of the harbor.

Broad Street had tiny old stores and small restaurants crammed together in a way that reminded Webb of photos of Europe. It had been strange, jumping off the interstate and going through the usual stretches of Walmarts and Home Depots and chain restaurants only to end up south of Broad, in a neighborhood that exuded old wealth and charm.

"Grasshopper requests permission to speak," Webb said as Lee eased the Camaro into one of the few parking spots on Broad. Webb was hoping a minor joke like that might lighten the mood inside the car.

"Yeah," Lee said. The lack of inflection in his voice reflected the somber mood that had cloaked him while they'd been cruising up and down the streets like tourists.

"Thinking about slaves while we were driving through those rich neighborhoods, weren't you?" Webb said. During Lee's shift at the steering wheel on the interstate, Webb had googled Charleston on the iPad. He'd learned that for a period of nearly a hundred years, before the Civil War, Charleston had been a hub for export based on an economy driven by cotton plantations. While Webb and Lee had driven along the quiet streets lined with glorious mansions, it hadn't been difficult for Webb to picture slaves inside the kitchens and dining rooms, serving people who had grown wealthy on the backs of slaves working the fields.

"Yeah," Lee said. "And wondering if much has really changed. Chains are different, that's all."

"I saw you leave a two-hundred-dollar tip at a restaurant," Webb said. "You'll be sitting me down for steak and lobster tonight. No chains on you."

Lee snorted. "Only because somewhere along the way, I broke them. Wasn't easy. Never is, for the poor."

"Poor whites too?" Webb asked.

Lee turned his head and didn't reply until he'd given Webb a long, thoughtful look. "Poor whites too."

"You spend time helping them?" Webb asked. "The poor whites? Or just poor blacks?"

"You and me are getting along pretty good," Lee said. "But that big foot of yours is about to step on the trigger of a land mine. Might want to back up a step."

"You live in a country where it's possible to break those chains," Webb said. "A country where you can try to help other people do the same. Isn't that something at least?"

"My self-imposed job is to get you to see the world my way," Lee said. "Not the other way around."

"Here's what I don't get," Webb said. "And first, let me make it clear: I agree that racism is crap. And if we agree, are you going to take a step my way and tell me it can be a two-way street? Blacks have to fight it as much as whites?"

"Hmmph," Lee said.

Webb thought that was as close as he would get to a yes from Lee, so he pushed on. "What I don't get is that I see you make judgments all the time. Me and my long hair for a negative judgment. Then the waitress and her short nails for a positive judgment. Want to explain that to me?"

"No," Lee said.

"So fun having thoughtful discussions with you," Webb said. "Answers like that make me want to keep putting my heart out on my sleeve for you."

Lee chuckled. "No, I don't want to answer it. Not yet. I want to give you a chance to answer it. When you are ready. It's a grasshopper thing."

"Wonderful," Webb said, clearly meaning the opposite.

"Deal with it," Lee answered. "Let's go talk to Derek Irvine."

Lee took a deep breath, and his body language changed from slumped to alert. A man going into battle.

They stepped out of the car. Across the street was a Starbucks. Not everything in old Charleston looked like it had been built two centuries earlier.

"Roy close by?" Webb asked as they walked. He had not caught a glimpse of the green Chevy half-ton for at least an hour.

"In combat in 'Nam," Lee said, "nobody on the other side ever saw him until it was too late for them. For a man as big as he is, he can be a ghost. He's around."

Webb liked that. It meant Ali was around too.

With light rain falling in the late-afternoon coolness, they reached the ancient wooden door of Antiques on Broad, varnished a rich brown, with ornate carvings of ships on the panels. It could have been there since before the Civil War. But not the security camera perched above it.

"Maybe we should invite Roy to steak and lobster," Webb said.

Which really meant maybe Lee should also invite Ali to steak and lobster.

"Focus, Daniel-san," Lee said.

"Wax on, wax off," Webb said, acknowledging he knew the source.

Both were lines from the movie *The Karate Kid*. The original. Not the remake. Webb didn't like the remake that much; it had a Justin Bieber song in it that drove him crazy. Maybe Webb would have to cut a song and call it "Never Play 'Never Say Never.'"

Lee gave Webb a grin and pushed the door open to the pleasant chiming of a bell.

The light inside was soft, from floor lamps scattered among the wardrobes, paintings, musty chairs and shelves of knickknacks.

A man in an elegant suit pushed himself toward them in a wheelchair. He had thin gray hair and square glasses; the skin of his face showed acne scars.

"Gentlemen," he said in a soft southern accent. If it seemed strange to him that an older black man and a kid with long hair and a Calgary Stampeders T-shirt were paired up to shop for antiques, nothing in his manner showed it.

"Mr. Derek Irvine," Lee said. "I'm Lee Knox. This is Jim Webb. We don't want to waste your time, so I won't pretend we're here for anything else but to ask you some questions about paddy fields and elephant grass and the Americans like you and me who did our best in a situation that made little sense then and makes less sense now."

"Not interested," Derek Irvine said. He rapped the top of his thighs with his knuckles, making a hollow sound. "Plastic all the way down. Other than telling you I lost both my legs over there and that the sound of grenades exploding still wakes me up in the middle of night, Vietnam is a subject I am reluctant to discuss. Even with another vet. The past is over."

No, Webb thought. It isn't.

"I understand," Lee said. "I lost plenty myself, so I have no intention of pushing you in that regard."

"Then we are finished here?"

"Yes," Lee said. "If you change your mind in the next couple of days, I've written my cell number on the back of this card."

Lee handed Derek a business card. Derek glanced at the handwritten number of Lee's throwaway cell on the back of the card and ran his fingers over the glossy raised ink on the front as he checked out the information.

"State Farm," Derek said, reading from the card. "Franklin, Tennessee. You should have called ahead and saved yourself a trip. This is a long ways to come to ask about a war that everyone else has forgotten."

He tapped the top of his thighs again and gave Webb a twisted, bitter smile. "Or that another generation knows nothing about."

"In the forties and fifties," Webb answered, "an obscure revolutionary named Ho Chi Minh fought, with the Viet Minh party, to overthrow French colonists in North Vietnam. His country was finally given official recognition by Russia and China, and a communist state was established when the Viet Minh succeeded in driving out the French. The United States and Great Britain gave official recognition to a French-backed State of Vietnam based in Saigon to the south. President Eisenhower's administration argued a domino theory— that if another country fell to communism, more would fall, and that meant they needed to stop North Vietnam from taking over the south. The irony is that Ho Chi Minh had first gone to American diplomats to get their support but had been ignored for nearly a decade. If he had been given help earlier, he wouldn't have embraced communism, because he was not driven by ideology but by a desire to help his people."

Webb spoke quickly, not giving either of the slack-jawed men a chance to interrupt. Since first meeting Lee and not having answers to any of Lee's questions about Vietnam, it had taken Webb hours on the web, sorting through the politics and history, to understand what had happened, and he wanted the satisfaction of slam-dunking this, as if he were reciting a short memorized piece to pass a classroom test.

"Rebels from the north began aiding rebels in the south against a puppet dictator supported by the Americans," Webb continued, "and the growing political unrest drove Americans from being unofficial observers helping the Army of the Republic of South Vietnam, or ARVN, to active involvement against the Viet Cong army from the north that had joined with the rebels among the villages of South Vietnam with a common goal of gaining complete independence. This turned into a war mainly fought by Americans because the ARVN wasn't that competent or inspired, and the rebel cause in the south was aided because American generals ignored on-the-ground advice and fought the same war that had been successful for them in World War II, using airplanes and bombs that more often than not destroyed the villages of the people they were trying to help."

It was a boring recital filled with too many facts, and Webb knew it. But he also knew it sounded impressive, like when you loaded up an essay to get a better grade.

"It made for a mixed-up, ugly situation where massive firepower lost a battle of attrition to guerrilla warfare," Webb continued. "Finally, the American people couldn't stomach continued losses of tens of thousands of young men halfway across the world for a cause that didn't seem important to anyone but politicians. America finally withdrew. It didn't help that the late sixties and early seventies was a time of great social unrest in America, with race riots in different cities and students at universities all across the country rebelling against the power of what they felt was an unfair establishment."

Webb finally stopped for breath. He gave the man in the wheelchair a calm smile and said, "That about cover it?"

"Dang," Lee said.

Irvine threw his head back and laughed with enthusiasm. Then he shook his head from side to side in wry admiration of Webb's slam dunk.

"All right," he said. "As long as it's nothing too personal, what questions can I try to answer for you gentlemen?"

# SEVENTEEN

They followed Derek as he wheeled into the back of the store and made a right-hand turn to move into a windowless office where there was a desk and a monitor. The desk had been modified so that the wheelchair fit in a space directly in front of the monitor and keyboard, leaving space on both sides for the papers strewn across the top. Two small chairs sat opposite it.

Derek made a tight turn with the wheelchair and sat behind his desk, motioning for Webb and Lee to take the chairs across from him.

Webb noted the photos on the walls as he sat. Mainly of a yacht, taken at different times of day.

Derek was on the deck in his wheelchair, his wife and children with him. The photos showed the family in different stages as the children grew older.

Yacht. So Derek had money. Plenty of it.

Webb guessed the antique shop didn't make Derek enough money to buy a yacht and figured that Derek came from a wealthy family. Maybe he'd grown up in one of the mansions south of Broad Street. Generations back, there'd have been slaves in the household.

Webb wondered if Lee was thinking the same thing about Derek's wealth, and it didn't take long to learn that the answer was yes.

"That's you as a boy?" Lee said. He pointed at a photo Webb hadn't noticed. There was a kid on the deck of the yacht, grinning against the sun. Standing on two sturdy, tanned legs.

"Better days," Derek said.

"Your family has been here a while?" Lee asked.

"Almost since Charleston was founded." Derek pronounced it *Chah-l-ston*. He smiled. "Half of what's in the antique shop comes from my aunts and uncles and their kids. I'm not in the business to make money. More like a hobby. Go back far enough in my family, you'll find pirates and smugglers."

And maybe slave traders, Webb thought. He waited for Lee to show some anger. Waited for Lee to say something like, "Go back far enough in my family, might be able to find slaves who worked for your family."

What Lee said, though, surprised Webb.

"Not a lot of officers put themselves in danger of getting hurt like you did, and I believe it would have been an honor to serve under your command," Lee said. "Your friends think you were crazy, signing up to serve our country?"

"I didn't believe in the war," Derek said. "Most of them didn't either. What we disagreed about was what it meant to serve. Military duty was a tradition in our family. Still is."

"They went to college and you went to the rice paddies," Lee said.

Derek nodded. "And I'm still trying to make sense of what happened there. My father served in Korea, and my grandfather in the Pacific against the Japanese. Seemed more clear, what they needed to do. Soldiers against soldiers. Not soldiers who often had no idea who the real enemy was in the next village. In 'Nam, we were boys, doing the best we could. That about sum it up?"

"Yeah," Lee said. "A lot better than the essay that Webb here just recited."

Webb shrugged. It had still been an impressive slam dunk.

"So how about you ask your questions," Derek said. "I don't mean this harshly, but there are still nights I wake up with the smell of nitrate in my nostrils, and the sooner we finish this, the better. Shrinks call it post-traumatic stress disorder and say you should talk it out. Me, I'm done talking."

Derek glanced at Webb, a good indication that it didn't make sense to him why Webb and Lee were the odd couple. "I don't even want to be curious about why you're asking these questions."

"Two men in your platoon," Lee said. "Jesse Lockewood and Casey Gardner. One died, one deserted. Anything you can tell me about either solider would be helpful."

Derek raised his eyebrows. "Maybe then I *am* curious about why you're asking these questions."

Derek looked at Webb and waited.

"My grandfather might have known Jesse Lockewood," Webb said. "My grandfather's dead, but I'm trying to figure some things out about his past.

Mr. Knox is a Purple Heart vet and has agreed to help me out."

"Don't need you trying to make me look good," Lee said to Webb. "Things I don't want to discuss either. I been through that stage already. No sleep. No eating. Just anger. Now, at least, I eat and sleep."

Derek still squinted at Webb, ignoring Lee.

"You're Canadian," Derek said.

Webb nodded.

"You said *oot* and *aboot*. Dead giveaway. Canadian tourists come in here all the time. We love them. Everybody loves Canadians."

"*Oot* and *aboot*?" Webb said.

Derek nodded. "You said you're trying to figure some things *oot aboot* your grandfather's past."

Webb thought it wasn't the time to mention that the person in the room with the real accent was the guy who turned any *r* in a word into an *h*, as in *Chah-l-ston*.

"I really didn't want to be curious about this," Derek told Webb, "but now I can't help it. How about this? If you find out anything worth knowing about Jesse Lockewood and Casey Gardner, you let me know. I've often wondered about those two."

"Yes, sir," Webb said. He was in the south. Calling Derek "sir" seemed natural.

"Something unusual made you wonder?" Lee said.

"I was the platoon sergeant," Derek said. "Both of them were in my squad. Our captain, Nathaniel Warwick, came from Albuquerque. He's a congressman now. Hope he's a better congressman than he was a captain. Lots of things fell on my shoulders that he should have handled."

Webb reminded himself that a platoon of thirty-six men had three squads of twelve.

"Nathaniel ignored advice, sent us into a firefight, trapped between Viet Cong pouring bullets at us from both sides," Derek said. "Almost like he wanted most of us to die. My radioman went down as we retreated, and the only way we could call in support from the air was to get that radio. Casey Gardner didn't hesitate. He was almost back with the radio when tracers found him. Jesse Lockewood ducked heavy fire and dragged Casey and the radio back to us. Made it back on one leg, dragging the other."

"Posthumous Bronze Star for Lockewood, right?" Lee said. "Gardner deserted."

"That's the official story," Derek said. "I never bought it entirely."

Derek ran his hands through his hair. Rubbed his neck. Looked up and to the right, closed his eyes briefly.

"Thing was," Derek said a few moments later, "both were taken away in the same medivac. To me, it looked like Gardner was bleeding out, and I never expected him to make it. Lockewood took some bullets in the calf of the leg he was dragging. That shouldn't kill a man. But word reached me that Lockewood died from infection two days later. And Gardner, he was true red and white and blue. He's the last guy I figured would bolt, but two weeks later, he's listed as a deserter. Of the two, I would have figured Jesse Lockewood to go native."

Lee asked the logical question. "Why's that?"

"A lot of soldiers made promises to Vietnamese women to get them stateside after the war, but when he was on leave, Lockewood guaranteed it for his girl by getting married in a Catholic ceremony, church and all. So if he died in action, she'd still be able to become an American. She had a name that wasn't easy to forget. Loan. Saigon family. Rumor had it she was connected to local gangsters. We liked to tease him about his gangster girl. Can't remember her first name, but the last name, Loan, that never struck me as Vietnamese, even though I later found out it wasn't uncommon over there. She had a younger brother."

Webb had two other identification cards in his pocket. The ones he had not left with Lee Knox to get destroyed in the house fire.

He reached into his pocket and pulled out the card with the photo of a Vietnamese woman on a Vietnamese national identity card.

"Quang Mai Loan?" Webb asked, reading the name beside the photo.

"Can only remember the last name," Derek said. "Sorry."

Webb handed the identification card to Derek, who didn't need to do much more than glance at it.

"That's her," Derek said, puzzled. "Jesse Lockewood's wife. Gangster girl."

# EIGHTEEN

A quiet restaurant overlooking harbor waters. The soft light of candles. A booth at a window. Ali across the table from Webb, her gorgeous face framed by long dark hair, a smile on her face as she gazed at him over a dish of succulent lobster.

The perfect evening.

Except for the fact that Roy Hawkins sat beside Ali and Lee Knox sat beside Webb.

Four of them. Not two.

Still, it was nice he'd been able to make Ali smile.

"Just so I understand," Webb had said, thinking about a recent email that someone had sent him with a top-ten list called Why Canadians Wonder About the United States, "here in America, politicians talk about the greed of the rich…at campaign-fundraising events where people pay $35,000 each for their dinner tickets?"

Lee wasn't smiling. He was groaning.

"Please, please," Lee said. "Don't get redneck Roy going on all this."

"You think it's redneck to be upset by Webb's question?" Roy said. He had a piece of steak on a fork, and he jabbed it at Lee. "Think about it. We have a black president and a black attorney general—two of the most powerful positions in government—and at the same time, twenty percent of the federal workplace is black when the general population of blacks is only fourteen percent. And you say government still discriminates against black Americans?"

"When blacks still have double the unemployment rate that whites do," Lee fired back, "I'd say we have a problem here."

"I have an idea," Ali said. "Why don't you two arm wrestle to see who's right?"

"Yuck," Roy said. "And hold hands with Lee? Cooties."

Lee settled—a bit. He finished a bite of steak and turned his attention to Webb. "You going to eat your lobster?"

Webb had had a few bites. Mainly he'd ordered it so that Lee would have to spend money. "Maybe later," Webb said. "Unless you want it."

Lee jabbed the lobster with his own fork and moved it onto his plate.

"You know what the problem is?" Lee said, cutting at the lobster. "Bumper-sticker armies. Complex arguments reduced to a sentence or two that hit people emotionally. We stop thinking about things and we stop discussing things and big issues get reduced to two sides, each shouting at the other."

"Amen," Roy said. "I'll agree with my buddy here on that one."

Lee jammed a piece of steak into his mouth and began to chew with enthusiasm.

"Even though," Webb said to Roy, "Lee just reduced the problem to a bumper-sticker statement that says bumper-sticker statements cause the problem?"

Roy stopped chewing and squinted at Webb.

"See?" Lee said to Roy. "That's what I have to deal with all day, driving with this kid. Today he asked me if I care about helping poor whites as much as I care about helping poor blacks."

Lee turned to Webb. "Here's my answer. I sell insurance to everybody."

"No," Roy groaned. "Not the insurance lecture."

"It's a nice bonus," Lee said, ignoring Roy. "My insurance business has helped me get ahead financially. But that's not the reason I'm in it. When I got out of the army, I was burning to do something about civil injustice. I didn't want to be one of those guys out there making speeches and looking for television time whenever the black community was treated unfairly, but someone who helped people in the community, even if it meant doing it under the radar. I figured if I could get poor families buying adequate insurance—help save them from insurance scams at the same time—it would make a big difference in their lives. Life insurance, health insurance, saving up money for college. It's not the system that's so bad, it's that those who don't know how to use the system don't get as far ahead as those who do use it. I'd rather see what I can do, one person at time."

Webb knew all about that. *Grasshopper, when you can snatch the pebble from my hand…*

Roy said, "In fairness, much as I hate his insurance lecture, I should point out that Lee's been known to pay insurance premiums for families, just to give them a head start."

Lee said, "I'm not the good guy here. Roy's been known to send me money for a fund for those families."

Ali said, "Isn't this cute? Now they're holding hands instead of arm wrestling. And all it took was for one to save the life of the other back in Vietnam for them to realize skin color doesn't matter."

For Webb, the banter felt good, like he was now part of a group. He wasn't normally a group person. Okay, until now he was never a group person.

"Enough about that," Lee said to Ali. "I promised to tell you about our day."

Lee took a few minutes to describe the meetings with Marcus Johnson and Matt Lockewood and Derek Irvine.

"Marcus got back to me," Lee said. "The contact they used in DC is a woman who works in Veterans Affairs. Webb and I are going to keep driving north and find out what we can from her. I think her position is too low-level to make her the Bogeyman. We need to find out who she talked to."

Webb began pushing his steak around his plate. He noticed that all of them were staring at him.

"Lee," Roy said, "when I was his age, that steak would have been gone in seconds. You been sneaking him snacks on the road?"

"It's probably a rock-star thing," Lee answered. "Stay skinny. Goes with the long hair."

Webb cut off a portion of his steak and dropped it onto Roy's plate. "Dive in. No sense letting it go to waste."

"Thanks," Roy said.

"Maybe you can answer a question while Roy finishes that steak," Webb said to Lee. "It's about Derek Irvine. You assumed he had a choice about going to war in Vietnam, and you assumed he would be an officer. Why?"

"I'll take this one," Roy said to Lee. "Otherwise Canuck boy here might assume you're prejudiced."

"And Canuck boy isn't a term of prejudice?" Ali said.

Roy waved away her objection and spoke to Webb. "During the war, the best way to avoid the draft was to stay in college. Meant most of the fighting was done by those of us too poor to have that option. And college kids and rich kids who did go tended to take officer training. Gave them a much higher survival rate. Drove us nuts, having some snooty kid with stripes, who knew nothing about the field, telling us what to do and costing lives in the process."

"Lots of them liked to lead from the back," Lee said. "Safer for them. Meet a vet in a wheelchair, like Derek Irvine, you know he wasn't out there waiting for grunts to clear a minefield for him."

"So," Webb said, pushing his plate away, "you'll tend to trust him when he remembers that Jesse Lockewood married a Vietnamese woman?"

Lee nodded.

"Then maybe I should show you some screen-shots I took on the iPad," Webb said. "Just before we drove into Gainesville."

"Screenshots?" Roy said.

"Daddy," Ali said, "you hold down the Home button and press the Power button at the same time. It takes a photo of whatever is on the screen."

"Home button?" Roy said, then grinned at Ali's pretended disgust.

"Lee was telling you that the Facebook account of Matt Lockewood's daughter disappeared not long after he shut the door on us," Webb said. "When Lee and I talked about it on the drive here to Charleston…"

Lee took the cue. "It was an easy conclusion that Matt Lockewood mentioned the Facebook connection to someone right after we talked to him. By telephone. Tells us his phone was tapped too. So one of the big questions is, who did he call? His daughter? Bogeyman? Bigger question is, why? What could be dangerous about someone like us seeing the Facebook account?"

A text pinged on Webb's iPhone. He glanced down and read it.

"I think I might have the answer," he said.

# NINETEEN

Webb held up his iPhone. "My cousin Adam put me in touch with a computer-geek friend of his named Leon. I've been texting him all day, asking for help. It just arrived. The questions I sent him were based on information from Matt Lockewood's daughter's Facebook account."

"That has disappeared," Lee said.

"Not exactly," Webb said.

Ali leaned forward. "Webby, if I'm guessing right, you took screenshots of her Facebook account?"

Webb liked that, her calling him Webby.

"And you're telling me now?" Lee said to Webb. "Thought we were a team."

"I'm just a simple grasshopper," Webb said.

Lee pulled out his iPad and searched the photo album. "I don't see any screenshots of Natasha's Facebook page."

"I emailed them to my photo account in the cloud and deleted them from the iPad," Webb answered. "They're safe if the iPad is stolen or lost."

Webb reached for the iPad. He used a web app to get to his photos. "Actually, Lee, nothing about the photos struck me as strange until we met Derek. I thought I'd bring this up over dinner for all of us to discuss."

Webb passed the iPad across the table to Roy. "Look at this. Notice anything unusual?"

Roy fumbled in his shirt pocket and pulled out a pair of reading glasses. "Not a word about old age," he warned Ali before he examined the photo.

"A team photo from twenty-five years ago to mark the anniversary of her nephew's state basket-ball championship," Roy said. "And a closeup photo of her nephew in a basketball uniform holding the trophy. Number twenty-five. This is a big deal why?"

He passed the iPad to Ali, who looked closely at the photo and said, "The team is called the Lindsay Thurber Bulldogs. Doesn't say what state." A slight smile crossed Ali's face. "Aaah, interesting. Lee, see if you can spot what my dad missed."

She passed the iPad back across to Lee, who said in a grumpy voice, "Roy, I need your reading glasses."

Roy sighed and handed them to Lee. Lee removed his own glasses, switched to Roy's and examined the photo.

"This kid, James McAuley," Lee said. "He doesn't look like his last name."

"I saw that," Roy said, "but this whole racism thing has me gun-shy."

"Kid looks Asian, doesn't he?" Webb said. "Like one of his parents was Asian and the other one wasn't. Want to guess if the mother or the father was Asian?"

Lee said, "Maybe her nephew James McAuley is the son of her brother Jesse Lockewood and McAuley's mother was once a gangster girl from Saigon? Yeah, I could see that happening. But why such a big deal that the account had to be erased once Matt Lockewood knew you'd seen it?"

"Do the math," Webb answered. "That photo is from a recent post. Twenty-five years ago, a kid old enough to play high-school basketball would have been born a few years after the Vietnam War."

"After?" Roy said. "But that would mean if Jesse Lockewood was the father…"

"…then Jesse Lockewood did not die in Vietnam," Ali said.

"Or," Lee said, "as a widow, she remarried here in the United States. Technically, Natasha Bartlett could still call the kid a nephew."

"Yes," Webb said, "but if that's all it is, why delete the Facebook account after Matt Lockewood found out we knew about it? If the kid is the son of someone else, there's nothing to hide. So what I'm thinking is that if we find James McAuley's father, we find Jesse Lockewood. And he can give us the answers we need."

"Seems like a long shot," Lee said.

Webb glanced at the information on his phone. "Lindsay Thurber is a high school in New Orleans. Same place that a professor Eric McAuley lives."

Webb read more. "I don't specifically know how Adam's friend found Eric McAuley—something about cracking a firewall and getting a phone bill and social security number. A social security number that belongs to a kid who died at age eight. Then there is eleven years of no activity, and suddenly activity again. Driver's license. School degrees. Credit cards. The kind of stuff you can find out with a credit check."

"Huh," Ali said reflectively. "You do a city- or state-wide search of records, find a kid born around the same time as you, who was registered as dead, then take his social security number and use that to build a new identity. If the dead kid is from out of state—"

"Utah," Webb said.

"Hardly any chance you'll be discovered using that social security number somewhere else," Ali finished.

Lee nodded. "New Orleans." He nodded again. "I think I have a way to get us there."

# TWENTY

It was four thirty in the morning. Originally, Webb and Lee had planned to head north to DC to talk to the woman in Veterans Affairs, hoping she might give them a lead on the Bogeyman. Phoning her was unthinkable; a phone call would almost certainly alert the Bogeyman they were on the way.

Now they'd changed their plans and were headed to a small airport north of Charleston; Roy and Ali would meet them in DC later that night, if all went well. The detour was taking them up Highway 17 to 701, through marshlands that smelled of seawater. Toward Myrtle Beach, South Carolina.

Lee was driving. It seemed like theirs was the only car on the road. In fact, it *was* the only car on the road: there were semitrucks but no cars.

The black Camaro, on the black pavement in the black of night beneath a clouded sky, felt like a mini spaceship whooshing on a charted course. Webb knew that spaceships didn't make any sound in outer space, because space was a vacuum, but he liked the analogy anyway. Strapped into the body-fitted leather front seat, hands on the wheel, the headlights of the semis like approaching comets...Webb was looking forward to his shift of driving, and he was going to miss the Camaro when all of this was over, however it ended.

Webb was wearing the Winnipeg Blue Bombers shirt again. When he'd left Nashville—just two days earlier but hundreds and hundreds of miles ago—he'd packed only one extra shirt, the Calgary Stampeders T-shirt. So in his hotel room after dinner the night before, he'd washed both in the sink and dried them with the hair dryer, knowing the alarm was set for so early, the shirts wouldn't dry just hanging on the shower rod with the underwear and socks he'd also washed.

"How come you haven't asked me a single question about what it was like to fight in Vietnam?" Lee said to Webb. "Most people do."

Webb didn't reply soon enough, because Lee's voice continued to come out of the darkness, the dashboard lights dimmed to almost nothing. "Or how come you haven't asked what happened in 'Nam when Roy saved my life, or later when I did the same for him?"

"Don't know you well enough," Webb finally said. "From what I understand about the war, you guys went through horrible things, things that cut deep and left bad memories. I figure a person needs to earn the right to ask about stuff like that, and I don't think I've earned it."

After a mile or so of silence, Lee said, "Makes me sad for you, son, that you understand something like that. I'm not asking about you and your stepfather, because I haven't earned the right. But just tell me this: is he the reason you understand?"

"He's the reason," Webb said. Webb liked that the Camaro's interior was so dark. This way, the conversation was just voices, not voices and faces. Still, Webb didn't offer any more to Lee than the flat answer he'd just given.

Webb wondered how much he wanted to share. He looked out the side window for a moment, but in his mind he saw his stepfather making him kneel on rice for five minutes, Webb's knees bare and the hard rice putting pressure points of agony on his knees.

"Your stepfather the reason you have nightmares?" Lee continued. "Yeah, I know it's a personal question. But every time you fall asleep in the car, you toss and turn and mumble and shout."

"My stepfather," Webb answered Lee, "is now out of my life and out of my mother's life. Nothing to worry about anymore." Webb almost told Lee about the last time he'd seen his stepfather. In Toronto, Webb had gone to the restaurant where he knew his stepfather had a reservation every day. Webb had knelt so that he was at eye level with his stepfather and had promised him that if he made even the slightest threat to Webb's mother, Webb would hunt him down. He'd seen just enough of a flicker of fear in his stepfather's eyes to know that they both knew Webb meant it.

"Maybe," Lee said softly, "just maybe, he was your tour of duty. Hear me out, okay?"

Webb let his silence speak for a willingness to listen.

"'Nam did that to a lot of us," Lee said. "Spend a long time under a lot of stress, it will hurt you long after. That's how it was for me. I was back on American soil, but angry all the time, like I wanted to hit people. I didn't sleep much. Wasn't interested in food. Just wanted to sit in a dark room and do nothing. Sound familiar?

"Remember what Derek said about his shrink?" Lee continued. "Today, people want to blame post-traumatic stress disorder for everything. Back then, no one knew what it was. Thing is, go through a tour of duty and it would be crazy to expect a person not to be a little crazy after it's over. What we found was the worst thing to do was pretend the craziness didn't exist. Once we understood there was a reason for it, the craziness made sense. To us and to them. It didn't get rid of the anger and nightmares right away, but you could deal with it, like dealing with a broken arm or leg, knowing it would eventually heal and that you weren't truly crazy and messed up."

"I'll be okay," Webb said.

"I know," Lee said. "But you'll be okay a little faster if you at least admit to yourself what's happening. If I were you, I'd cut the hair. Why remind yourself every time you look in the mirror that you still have to rebel against your stepfather? Don't allow him that hold on you, especially if he's up in Canada and you're down here. Don't allow him that kind of hold on you even if you live in the same house. Find someone to talk to about what happened. That's a good way to let some of the stress leak out and disappear."

As Webb watched the streaking comets from the semitrucks on the opposite side of the highway and thought about Lee's advice, he was glad that Lee gave him silence for the rest of their drive in the dark.

# TWENTY-ONE

From what Webb could see in the dawn's light, the Conway-Horry County Airport consisted of half a dozen buildings on one side of a single runway, set in a long swath that had been cut into a dense grove of trees.

Twenty or so small airplanes were parked on pavement to the side of the runway. Lee drove up to a low, flat building with wide-open doors. The building was large enough for three small airplanes to be parked inside.

Lee wheeled the Camaro directly into the building and snapped off the ignition.

"Let's stay put and watch the fun," Lee said to Webb. "Niner's got some kind of temper on him."

"Niner?" Webb said. "Didn't you say his name was Wayne Mason?"

"Grasshopper," Lee answered. "Watch, listen and learn."

Within thirty seconds, a short man in dirty cover-alls came out from behind one of the airplanes and marched toward the Camaro. His thinning hair was red, mixed with plenty of gray. He was carrying an aluminum baseball bat.

"Keep in mind," Lee said, "we have tinted glass. Niner won't be able to see inside our windows. Grab your phone and get video of this."

Niner stared at the car for a few seconds, as if he was waiting for someone to get out. Webb began to record with his iPhone.

"Hey," Niner shouted when he decided that no one was stepping out. "Get that piece of crap out of my hangar before I smash it to pieces."

He lifted the bat.

"Count his fingers," Lee said to Webb. "We were in Saigon on leave and he was leaning with his hand on the roof of a taxi. Someone shut the door, and the cab driver took off fast. Nobody except Niner knew that the door had slammed on his pinkie. Tore it right off his hand. Never did find the finger."

Niner's fingers were wrapped around the bat handle. Sure enough, Webb saw a stub where Niner's little finger should have been. Nine fingers. Niner.

"I said, get that piece of dog poop out of my hangar!" Niner was screaming now, some spit spraying from his mouth.

"In about a minute," Lee said, "he'll have worked himself up enough to start smashing our headlights. Let's see if I can get his blood pressure really going."

Lee hit the horn and held it for about ten seconds.

Niner's eyes started bulging, and he let rip with a string of curses that included words Webb didn't even fully understand.

As Niner kept going, Lee said, "Only thing you can do is wait until he runs out of air."

When Niner took a much-needed breath, Lee pushed open his door and yelled, "Put a sock in it, Niner."

"What the…?" Niner said.

Lee stepped out of the car, laughing. "Dang, I wish I had that on video. No wait, I do have it on video."

"Lee? You son of a—"

"Good to see you, Niner," Lee said. "You still shanking the ball a couple times a round?"

"Lee Knox," Niner said, grinning now. "You'd find out if you ever delivered on your promise to golf Myrtle Beach with me. I got the morning open, if you want."

Niner dropped the bat, and it pinged on the concrete. He stepped forward and wrapped his arms around Lee's belly, lifted the larger man off the ground in a hug and then set him down.

Webb stepped out the passenger side.

"Niner, meet Webb," Lee said.

Niner looked at Webb with suspicion and said to Lee, "You picking up road trash these days?"

"It's your hair," Lee told Webb. "Niner still hasn't got past the hippie days."

"Drug-smoking, flag-burning, long-haired..." Niner let fly with a bunch of imaginative swear words.

When Niner had to draw breath again, Lee said, "Niner, go easy on the kid. He's the one that took the video of you and your baseball bat. If he puts it on YouTube, you're going to have a million people laughing at you, not just me."

Once more, Niner was off and running. Webb found it amazing that Niner had not repeated a single curse the entire time. When Niner came up for air, Lee said to Webb, "We'd do this all the time in Saigon. Was the best entertainment we had, right, Niner?"

Niner kept squinting at Webb in suspicion. "Look at him, Lee. Just like one of those university protesters who let us go to 'Nam and do the dirty work."

"Niner," Lee said, "he's a good kid. Really. You should listen to him on guitar. Webb, why don't you play a song for Niner?"

"Nope," Webb said. "I'm not a trained monkey."

"See, Niner? The kid's not easy to push around. It's why he's growing on me. Now, how about you settle down and let me ask you for a favor?"

"A good kid?" Niner said. "You'll vouch for him?"

"Yup," Lee said. "I'm here because someone burned my house down, and Webb's helping me find out who did it."

Niner walked to Webb and stuck out a hand. "Then nice to meet you."

Webb accepted the grave and serious handshake, getting the impression that Niner had no middle ground and now Webb was on his good side.

Niner said to Lee, "Only favor I can do for you that others can't, I'm guessing, is transportation. I'm all yours. Plane can be ready in twenty minutes. Just need to do preflight."

Webb hated asking anyone for a favor. He marveled that a man like Niner would drop everything to help an old war buddy, no questions asked. Must be a nice feeling, being part of something like that.

"I need to register a flight plan," Niner said. "Where we headed?"

"New Orleans," Lee said. "Lakefront Airport."

"Hey, Smitty's in New Orleans. Heard he got remarried. Some girl half his age, built like a—"

"Heard the same thing," Lee said. "But we can't meet Smitty. Need to keep this quiet."

"Too bad. What I heard about his wife was—"

"All business, Niner. Best if you didn't even get out of the airplane."

"I could've picked you up in Tennessee," Niner said. "It's not far out of the way from here."

"I couldn't call ahead," Lee said. "Worried that your phone might be tapped. Same reason I'm wondering if you might be able to list Baton Rouge on your flight plan, and we divert to New Orleans on short notice."

"Done," Niner said. "You want to stay under the radar." He grinned. "Literally."

"Exactly," Lee said. "No credit cards and no ATMs. Brought my checkbook though, and I'll cover the expenses. It would be helpful if you waited a few days to cash my check. I'll tell you the whole story while we're in the air."

"I won't take a dime for this," Niner said.

"Niner…"

"Unless you agree to that," Niner said, "you're going to drive to New Orleans. Friends don't pay friends for help."

# TWENTY-TWO

The airplane was a 1962 Beechcraft Bonanza P35, capable of a cruising speed of 150 knots per hour—which, Niner explained, was just over 170 miles per hour. It was cherry-red and, gleaming in the sunlight, it looked new. The interior was all polished hardwood and leather.

Webb liked it. A lot. And he liked the sense of movement. They were headed south and west, to the Gulf Coast.

Lee and Niner shared the cockpit, talking over the headsets, and that left Webb some solitude in the back. He pulled the Baby Taylor out of his bag and started strumming and picking. Six strings, and he could pick any one or any combination with his right hand. Left hand on the neck, forming more combinations, holding the strings down against a fret, then sliding down to a new combination on a lower fret. He did it automatically, with barely any more thought than it took to lift a foot to take a step. That's what you needed to do—play for hours and hours and countless hours, until your brain didn't need to direct your hands and only needed to decide what note was to be played. Walking was no different. The brain didn't tell the feet how to walk; it only decided where it wanted the feet to take the body.

For years, Webb had done exactly what he was doing now: letting his fingers roam the guitar neck and strings. He'd done it watching television, repeating a single riff endlessly while he learned the rhythms, feeling the song. Webb didn't talk much about what was inside him, but it poured out when he held a guitar.

They were flying at an altitude where vehicles were mere dots on the highways, and the forests looked like carpet. Lakes like mud puddles of various colors glinted in the sun as they headed southwest.

Niner had said it would take about five hours, that they'd be bucking a headwind typical for late December. They'd have to stop for fuel once, a couple of hours short of New Orleans.

Webb liked having this time alone in the back of the airplane, looking out the window as he experimented with some new riffs. Thing was, he couldn't get that song out of his head.

*There won't be any trumpets blowing / come the judgment day / On the bloody morning after / one tin soldier rides away.*

Webb began to experiment with a minor key, adding some darkness to the melody, changing up the rhythm a bit. He liked it, got lost in it. He was startled when the engine of the plane changed pitch, and he glanced out the window to see the tops of houses as they skimmed toward a landing.

Niner put the Beechcraft down like he was settling a kitten onto a pillow, turned the plane at the end of the runway and taxied back to the fuel pumps.

All of them got out and stretched. It was already 10:00 AM. The day had begun in Charleston, taken them almost to Myrtle Beach and now they were—Webb pulled up a travel app on his iPhone—in the heart of

Alabama again, a city called Dothan. He tilted his face to a warm breeze. Felt Lee's hand on his shoulder.

"Niner says he wants you at the controls once we get up. You okay with that? Flying this?"

"Very," Webb said.

"Good," Lee said. "As soon as we're ready, you take the copilot seat. I'm going to have a good snooze in the back."

Ten minutes later, Webb was in the headset, communicating with Niner by microphone.

Niner taxied again, taking the plane to the end of the runway, then turning it.

"Take off and land into the wind," Niner said. "Gives extra lift. We want a wind speed of about one hundred and five to get airborne. Breeze is into us at fifteen miles an hour. Means we only need ninety miles an hour of ground speed."

Webb nodded. There were pedals at his feet, a yoke in front of him.

Niner gave the engine a surge, and the Beechcraft accelerated, making the edges of the runway seem to converge.

Then the Beechcraft tilted upward, and Webb was staring at clouds. An amazing sensation of freedom.

Niner spent twenty minutes explaining the controls to Webb. When he was satisfied that Webb understood the principles behind flying and the principles behind the controls, he gave Webb a thumbs-up.

"Take us in some gentle banks and turns," Niner said. "See if you can do it without waking Lee. It's kind of like driving. Best way to do it is to imagine an egg in a little bowl on the dash. You never want to turn or stop or take off so fast that the egg rolls out."

The sense of power Webb felt maneuvering the Beechcraft thrilled him. It was better than driving the Camaro.

"Excellent," Niner said. "Now take it down a little."

Webb pointed the nose downward. Land filled most of the windshield. He loved it.

"Up."

Slight acceleration and sky replaced the view of land. The Beechcraft seemed like an extension of Webb's body. *Too cool.*

Niner glanced back at Lee. "He's strapped in," Niner said. "And you put your bag under the seat like I asked. I want to take over the controls, because now it's time for a little payback."

"Payback?"

"Remember how you videoed me on your iPhone when I was screaming at the Camaro because I didn't know who was inside? Do me a favor and get ready to take more video. But you're going to have to hang on tight to your phone."

"Tight?" Webb put the iPhone into video mode.

"Don't drop it."

"Tight," Webb confirmed.

"Start now, and make sure you keep the camera on him."

Webb turned and picked up Lee on the screen. Lee was already asleep, leaning back, strapped in tight in case of turbulence.

Niner tilted the airplane nose up so that it was riding vertical to the ground instead of horizontal.

Even with the headset covering his ears, Webb could hear Lee's scream of terror. Webb felt a little puckered in the butt himself, but he kept the video going, capturing Lee's wide-open eyes.

Lee's scream rose in pitch as Niner put the airplane completely upside down and flew horizontal to the ground again.

Webb was doing his best not to scream. He glanced over at Niner, whose short hair was hanging straight down. Niner had a huge grin on his face.

Niner put the plane right-side up again, and Webb was able to breathe. Niner jerked a thumb in Lee's direction.

"Look at him cussing me out," Niner said. "Make sure you get that on video too."

# TWENTY-THREE

"We're good?" Niner asked Lee.

"Except I need to empty my shorts," Lee said. "I should have been wearing diapers when you did that trick flying."

They all laughed.

The three of them were on the runway beside the Beechcraft, sun baking the asphalt. Hot day for late December, the guy at the fuel tank had said. Niner had first circled downtown New Orleans for Webb, giving him a view of the Mississippi and showing where it branched out south of New Orleans into a massive delta that looked like broccoli. Then he had taken them down over the gray, flat waters of Lake Pontchartrain, the huge estuary fed by freshwater rivers but connected to the Gulf of Mexico.

They'd landed at Lakefront Airport, which was on a peninsula at the south end of Lake Pontchartrain, and it had felt to Webb that as they came in over the water, the landing gear should kick up spray.

"We're good," Lee said. "We've got water and chocolate bars and a couple of empty Coke bottles. Thanks for arranging the loaner."

At private airports, Niner explained, there was often a vehicle or two for out-of-town pilots to use on an informal basis. This one was a battered blue Ford Taurus, probably ten years old, but if anybody wanted to complain, they were welcome to rent a car instead. Lee said he liked the Taurus, because it was so anonymous and otherwise they'd have had to use a credit card for a rental. They still didn't have any idea how many of Lee's Vietnam friends were being tracked by the Bogeyman.

"I'll wait in Baton Rouge as long as I need to," Niner said. "You whistle, I'll be back here in a jiffy."

An hour outside of New Orleans, Niner had radioed in the change in flight plan, saying he needed to get some fuel before resuming the journey, just in case the Bogeyman had been monitoring and had sent people ahead to Baton Rouge.

"I owe you," Lee said.

"Nope," Niner said. "We don't do things like this to build up debts."

Niner saluted Web and said, "Get a haircut, hippie."

Then Niner grinned and hopped into the airplane.

Webb was grinning too as he and Lee walked to the Taurus.

"You drive," Lee said. "I'll navigate. No offense to a workhorse like the Taurus, but the handling of it is going to feel soggy compared to the Camaro, and I'll let you deal with the wet-noodle turns."

Webb noticed the difference as they drove away from the airport, but he didn't care. They were closing in on Jesse Lockewood. He hoped.

They had an address on Chartres Street, in the French Quarter. Lee directed Webb past the grounds of the University of New Orleans, palmettos obscuring the square white buildings. Then they turned south down an avenue called St. Bernard, which ran underneath an interstate, past houses built sideways to the street, past an old whitewashed church, beneath another interstate, then through neighborhoods with cars on blocks and finally to mansions with lawns trimmed to perfection.

"Tiny houses," Webb said, making a joke as they neared the heart of the downtown. He pointed to some small white buildings crowded together in a park.

Lee snorted. "Cities of the dead, you mean. Those are above-ground vaults for burials. This city, the water table is too high. Can't put coffins in the ground."

Webb couldn't help himself. *Cities of the dead.* Cool phrase, he thought. He'd need to go to iTunes and see if someone had already used it. If not, he could build a song off something like that. Then he realized he was actually thinking about a song again, actually wanting to write. Not a bad feeling.

"We turn left in about a block," Lee said, cutting into Webb's thoughts. "You liking these old buildings?"

The buildings were two and three and four stories tall, all of them with ornate iron balconies, some with plants cascading down almost to the streets.

"This is a good time to visit," Lee said. "Other times in the French Quarter, you can't walk without having to turn sideways, it's so crowded. Always liked the vibe in this city. Great music, great food."

At the steering wheel, Webb turned as directed at the next corner.

"Keep your eyes open for a convent," Lee said. "The address is across the street. New Orleans is a city of contrasts. Convents on one corner, blues bars on the other."

As Webb made the final turn, the street opened up ahead, and it looked like a barge was blocking the road until Webb realized the street ended in a T at the banks of the Mississippi, and the barge was on the waters ahead of them.

"Here," Lee said.

They parked in front of a building that looked like it had been there since the time of pirates. Dull red brick, stone tiles on the roof, gargoyles in the corners.

"Just like this?" Webb said, gesturing at the ancient wooden doors of the separate apartment units at ground level. "We walk up and knock?"

"Just like this," Lee answered, understanding Webb's comment. "If he's home, he's home. Otherwise, we wait. If he's who we think he is, the man's been on the run since the Vietnam War. He'll be skittish, and phoning won't do anything but give him a chance to run again."

Nobody answered the door.

Lee shrugged. "Plan B then. Back to the car. Empty Coke bottles."

Plan B was to wait and watch for as long as it took. Without leaving even for a moment. The Coke bottles they'd plucked out of a recycling bin up at the airport were for bathroom breaks. Gross, Lee had said, but necessary. Webb was glad the empties had screw-on caps.

They sat in the Taurus. Windows down, radio tuned to a jazz station, breeze keeping them cool as they watched the sidewalks.

"Hard to imagine a city like this flooded so high that bodies floated down the streets," Lee said. "Not when you see it now on a pretty day like today. You know who bore the brunt of Hurricane Katrina, don't you? Wasn't the people who could drive away from the flood warnings in their big suvs. No sir."

Webb remembered all the news stories about that hurricane.

"Folks put the blame in lots of places for the levees that broke and the dikes that collapsed," Lee said. "Media liked sending out images of people gathered in the Superdome and all that went wrong there. But what really gets me is how the poor—and by poor, I mean mainly black—weren't able to rebuild after. And you know why?"

"Yup," Webb said.

"Huh?" Lee had obviously expected to go on with his little lecture.

"Insurance," Webb said. "That's what you were going to say, wasn't it? Get the poor to set aside just a little of their money for insurance and that'll take care of them better than government."

Lee's face had the crinkled look of a puzzled basset hound. Then he broke into a grin of admiration. "Dang. You do listen."

"I am but your humble servant," Webb said.

Lee began to laugh, but then froze. "Look!"

And there he was. Grocery bag in his arm, walking up the sidewalk, maybe thirty paces away.

Jesse Lockewood. Four decades older than the photo on the military identification card. But still him, beyond mistake. A man who was supposed to have been killed in battle, placed in a body bag and flown home for burial.

# TWENTY-FOUR

Lee stepped out of the car, stretching. Just like someone who'd been napping for a while, not someone in predator mode.

Now only a couple of paces away, Eric McAuley—Webb still thought of him as Jesse Lockewood—barely glanced at Lee.

McAuley had taken good care of himself over the decades. His hair was silvered at the edges, and his jaw was square and the skin tight. He was tanned, and his khaki pants and light green golf shirt made him look like he golfed.

He could be a successful businessman or maybe someone who ran a restaurant in the French Quarter. Or he could just as easily be a popular university professor teaching English literature based on a hard-earned PhD.

Thanks to information from his cousin Adam's geek friend, Webb knew, of course, that Eric McAuley actually did teach at the University of New Orleans and that the online staff photo showed an icon of Shakespeare instead of McAuley himself.

Lee made no threatening moves as McAuley neared the old Taurus. Lee simply remained leaning against the door and said two words. "Jesse Lockewood."

McAuley didn't flinch. Didn't break his stride. Didn't even look at Lee.

"Bad acting," Lee said to McAuley's back. "Anyone else would have looked over, wondering why I got their name wrong. You want a quiet talk with me and my friend over coffee and beignets? Or you want to leave behind this nice life as Eric McAuley and start running again as Jesse Lockewood?"

McAuley kept walking.

Webb stepped out of the car too.

"You're closing in on sixty," Lee said, raising his voice slightly because of the distance McAuley kept adding. "Think it's going to be easy to rebuild?"

McAuley stopped, as if considering Lee's words, then turned. "I'm putting my groceries inside. I'll be back. That okay with you?"

"Okay with us," Lee said. "I'm not here to force you to do anything. No weapons, no threats. Just want to talk, and then my friend and I will be out of your life. What you'll get out of it is knowing how we found you, and the steps you can take to make sure that Vietnam doesn't catch up to you again."

The answer must have satisfied McAuley, because after he opened the door and stepped inside his apartment, he was back out in less than two minutes.

"Let's walk," he said. Nothing about his body language suggested he was afraid. "Nice café around the corner. I don't want my wife involved."

He glanced at Webb, who could see McAuley's eyes taking in the long hair.

"I know, I know," Webb said. "Hippie. That's the first thing you Vietnam vets think."

"No," McAuley said. "Your face. Something familiar about it. It'll come to me." McAuley turned to Lee. "Beignets? You've been to New Orleans before."

Lee grinned. "Love those things. Great on your lips. Stay on your hips."

All three remained silent the remainder of the short walk around the corner. A waiter greeted McAuley by name and showed them to a sunny spot on the patio. McAuley ordered beignets and coffee for all of them. It was very civilized, considering that someone had burned down Lee's house because of the man across from them.

"I'm Lee Knox," Lee said. "Former second lieutenant. Thirty-eighth Infantry."

"The Cyclones," McAuley said. "Amazing how that stuff never leaves your brain, remembering names for divisions."

McAuley gave Webb another questioning glance.

"Jim Webb," Webb said.

McAuley studied them some more. "I've always had an escape plan. Reason I didn't run when you called out my name was because of sheer curiosity. Not only about how you found me, but this whole odd-couple thing between the two of you. That curiosity is only growing. One of you talks like a Minnesotan. The other like the south."

"Black and white," Webb said. "Something Lee keeps pointing out."

"Webb's Canada," Lee said. "I'm Tennessee. And he's the one who started it. A friend of a friend kind of thing. Webb had questions about two names and one photo. Jesse Lockewood and Benjamin Moody."

McAuley looked at Webb. "That's where I've seen you before. Sean Alexander. Same features."

Sean Alexander. Hearing the name from someone else was like a zap of electricity to Webb.

"My grandfather," Webb said.

"I hope he died a horrible death," McAuley said. His face tightened. "And please, do take offense. I thought this was going to be a friendly chat, and I hoped we could work things out, but after what that man did to me, I'd gladly dump your body in a swamp."

Their waiter brought the beignets and coffee in a pot on a tray and set it down.

McAuley's expression stayed tight, as if he was clenching his jaw. He ignored the beignets and didn't move his gaze away from Webb.

"Wow, these are great," Lee said, his mouth full. "Deep fried and sugared. We can order some to go, right?"

Webb's gut was churning. He kept hearing McAuley's words about Webb's grandfather. *After what that man did to me...*

"Hey, Lockewood," Lee said to McAuley when neither Webb nor McAuley broke off the stare-down. "Ease off. Webb's not responsible for his grandfather's actions."

McAuley turned a slow gaze toward Lee. Then he gave a puzzled frown as Lee pulled out his wallet and put a hundred-dollar bill on the table, right beside the coffee pot.

"Here's what I have—straight-up odds—that says you're wrong about the kid's grandfather," Lee said. "Someone else did you wrong, and that's why I'm here. For payback against the same person. Want to take the bet?"

McAuley relaxed, but only slightly. "What do you know?"

"The kid's grandfather has passed on," Lee said. "Yet someone burned my house down a few days ago. I like the odds that a dead man wasn't the one to either burn down my house or send someone to do it. So whatever happened, you should assume someone else was responsible and is trying to bury the past. Webb and I think of him as the Bogeyman, and we're trying to find him for some payback."

Lee said to Webb, "You've never been to New Orleans before, right? Try a beignet. Don't let Lockewood spoil your appetite with an unfounded accusation. There's still a lot of digging to do before we find out what really happened, and in America we're supposed to believe in the innocent-until-proven-guilty thing."

Webb took Lee's advice and set his iPhone on top of the hundred-dollar bill. He grabbed a beignet and took a bite. It tasted better than he expected.

"Someone wanted your military ID cards destroyed," Lee said to McAuley. "That's why they torched my house. It worked." He pointed at the iPhone on the bill. "Except the kid here was smart enough to take photos of the cards. Want to see them?"

"No," McAuley said. "I know what they look like. Last man who had them was this kid's grandfather. Sean Alexander. I traded them to him so that my wife and I could escape Saigon. We didn't get too far."

McAuley's face twisted slightly with bitterness. "We didn't get too far with Sean Alexander's help anyway. We had to get here on our own. And apparently, as your presence indicates, that still wasn't far enough."

"Sounds like quite a story," Lee said. "How about you make another trade? Your story for Webb's story and my story about how we found you. When we're finished, maybe you'll owe the kid an apology."

"Fair enough," McAuley said. "In a small town in the southern part of Vietnam, I saw someone counting diamonds in a tent. That's where it began."

# TWENTY-FIVE

Dawn brought them into the hills of the Shenandoah Valley, gray with trees that had long lost their leaves to the cold. Occasional snowflakes blew across the windshield.

The night before, because Lee didn't want Niner involved in a flight plan taking them anywhere close to DC, they'd taken a commercial jet from New Orleans to Richmond, Virginia. They'd learned enough from Eric McAuley to get a sense of who was after them and why. Staying under the radar didn't matter so much anymore. They could have flown directly into DC, but if they were being tracked, they wanted to make it look like they were still trying to hide.

"Cold," Lee said. "Too cold for how we are dressed."

"Can hardly see through this blizzard," Webb answered. He was back to the Blue Bombers T-shirt and missing his collection. Normally, he'd be wearing a Hamilton Tiger Cats shirt at this point in the rotation. Black and gold and white. Eight championships. Fans almost as tough as the football players, looking down their noses at the sissies who cheered for the Toronto Argonauts just down the road while the Argonauts fans scoffed at the iron-workers from Hamilton.

Webb was driving a Dodge Charger that Lee had rented at the Richmond airport before finding a nearby motel. Webb loved the responsiveness of the throttle, and the way the vehicle shifted at the slightest nudge of the steering wheel. Hard to choose which he'd take—Camaro or Charger—but that was only in a fantasy world, because his only real option was a bus pass. He tried telling himself that a diesel bus had plenty more horsepower than the Charger, but that didn't cheer him up.

"Blizzard? Don't go sarcastic Canadian on me here," Lee said. "With luck, Laura Andrews is going to meet us at the Vietnam Veterans Memorial. Washington's a lot colder than Charleston was. You'll be standing around in a T-shirt."

That was the plan. Lee had called Ali and Roy the day before from New Orleans, with instructions for Ali to go to the Veterans Affairs office and give Laura Andrews a note requesting a meeting this morning. Lee wanted it to look like they were trying to set up the meeting outdoors, where they couldn't get trapped or have someone electronically spy on their conversation. If she insisted on meeting inside somewhere, that would tell them the bait had been taken.

"I'm okay," Webb said. "I've shivered before."

"Not worried about how you're going to feel. Worried about how it will draw attention to you if you're the only one there not wearing a coat. How about we make a quick stop in the next town to get you some winter clothing?"

"Let's find a Goodwill store or a Salvation Army. You're paying for gas and hotels and meals and—"

"Maybe I didn't make this clear earlier, and I apologize. If I can nail whoever burned down my house, my insurance company is not going to have to pay out on my home policy because they'll make the person responsible for it cover the cost. Everything I spend on the road is a business expense, and I'll get it back, including a winter coat for you. We do this right, and the insurance company might even cut you a check for acting as my private investigator."

"Winter coat sounds good," Webb told him with a grin.

Three hours later, with Lee driving, they crossed the Potomac River, a sharp wind riffling the surface of the water. A United Airlines jet swooped past above them, on a flight path to the airport runways on the west side of the river.

Ahead, stark and beautiful, was the obelisk of the Washington Monument, and then, minutes later, the rotunda.

Webb was waiting for Lee to bring up the famous peace march that had sent a hundred thousand people into the open area in 1963. He'd been googling famous civil-rights events to try to be one step ahead of Lee.

Instead, when they reached the Vietnam War Memorial, Webb understood why Lee had been silent since crossing the river, silent while parking the car, silent while walking toward the memorial. Webb had been grateful for the down jacket that protected him from a cutting wind during that walk.

The Vietnam Veterans Memorial was near the Lincoln Memorial. It consisted of two long walls, each about ninety steps long, sunk into the ground, with earth built up behind them. One wall pointed at the Washington Monument, and the other at the Lincoln Memorial. Where they connected at a right angle, they were over ten feet tall, tapering from there so that the ends of each wall were only eight inches high.

The granite was polished, and Webb saw his and Lee's reflection as they looked at the names. More than fifty-eight thousand names. Soldiers killed in action or missing in action.

More than fifty-eight thousand.

Webb looked at the granite. The reflective aspect had been deliberate. So that people would see themselves and think about their role as survivors? So they would see themselves and wonder if humanity would always be like this? Maybe Lee was right. Change needed to happen, but it could only be done one person at a time. Words from the song drifted through his thoughts.

*There won't be any trumpets blowing*
*Come the judgment day*
*On the bloody morning after*
*One tin soldier rides away.*

"We need to stay together," Lee said as he stared at a row of engraved names. "In the note, there were instructions for Laura to look for a kid with long hair with a black guy. We gave her a one-hour window to find us here."

They'd already discussed whether she might be followed. What was more crucial, Lee argued, was whether she would show up at all and whether she would feel like helping them.

Webb stayed close to Lee as he walked slowly along the wall, looking at names but with an expression on his face that said he was seeing soldiers torn by bullets and fragmentation grenades.

Webb kept his silence too.

He thought Lee was looking for names of men in his platoon, so was surprised when Lee reached out and pointed at a name: Jesse Lockewood.

Lee kept going along the wall. Slowly. It staggered Webb how many names were up there. It was one thing to hear about the deaths of thousands of soldiers and think of it as a statistic. *More than fifty-eight thousand.* It was another thing to see name after name and feel the impact of understanding how much of a tragedy each death was for the mothers and fathers and brothers and sisters and husbands and wives and sons and daughters and friends who had to bury the soldier.

About ten minutes after they'd found Jesse Lockewood's name on the memorial, Webb saw a small woman approaching furtively, bundled up and with a scarf over her head. There weren't many people at the memorial because of the weather, and she was easy to spot.

Wisps of reddish hair blew out from under the scarf. She was wearing a long coat and had flat-heeled boots that nodded to sensibility instead of fashion.

She and Webb locked eyes.

She knew he was looking for her. He knew she was looking for them.

"Lee," Webb said, tapping Lee on the shoulder. "Laura's here."

# TWENTY-SIX

Warmth. Cinnamon latte.

At the Memorial Wall, those had been Laura Andrews' two conditions for a continued conversation. She'd wanted them to go indoors.

She was cupping her hands around a mug, blowing steam off the top of the latte. She'd taken off her jacket and hung it from a coatrack. She was wearing a brown polyester business suit. The polish on her fingernails was chipped, and the forefinger of her right hand was stained with nicotine.

"I don't get all this cloak-and-dagger stuff," Laura started. Her voice was longtime-smoker raspy.

"You could have called me at the office instead of sending a note that said secrets would be released to the *Washington Post* if I didn't go to the memorial on my lunch break and look for the two of you."

Lee had an untouched coffee in front of him. Webb was drinking orange juice. He'd already had too many coffees since the alarm went off at 6:00 AM.

"By the way," she said, "the request on the note to bring the file on Jesse Lockewood? Not a chance. I don't break rules. I need my job."

That, Webb guessed, was why she'd come to the memorial in the first place. Afraid that secrets sent to the *Washington Post* would cost her that job. It meant she was a very close link to the Bogeyman.

Lee must have realized it too.

Lee said, "We don't aim to to get you into trouble."

"I haven't done anything wrong," she said. "If this is about Jesse Lockewood, I was responding to an official request from authorized military personnel. On the other hand, I have no idea who you are, so don't expect I'm going to share any information with you. I just came here to find out why you thought there was some kind of secret the newspaper would be interested in."

"I'm the one who initially wanted information about Jesse Lockewood," Lee said. "I asked a friend, who asked a friend, who asked another friend. And the third friend turned out to have the authority to make the call to you."

Laura straightened in her seat. "I'm not responsible for any leaks from the person who had the authorization."

"Let's just say his name, okay?" Lee said. "General Sutton. Out of the air base in Atlanta. He's the one who called you to ask about Jesse Lockewood's file."

"I can neither confirm nor deny," she said.

"Fair enough," Lee said. "What you should know is that within hours of someone reaching out to you to ask about Jesse Lockewood, my house was burned to the ground. I doubt that was coincidence. I think whoever started the fire wanted to destroy a military identification card with Jesse Lockewood's photo on it."

"I doubt anyone could make that connection with certainty," she said. "Houses catch on fire. You have my sympathy."

"There's more to it than that," Lee said. "But I only share it on a need-to-know basis. I'm sure you can respect that."

"I can tell you that it doesn't matter to me," Laura said. "I have a desk job and that's all I worry about. What is in front of me on my desk. At the end of the day, I don't even worry about that anymore until I get back to my desk the next morning. In fifteen years, I will retire with benefits—that's what matters to me."

"All I want to know," Lee said, "is if there was anything out of the ordinary in Jesse Lockewood's file. If there were any notes or flags on it. If Lockewood was involved with an intelligence agency of any kind or was under investigation by the military police."

She looked away, obviously wanting to avoid eye contact with Lee. Then she looked back. "Nothing."

She wasn't a good liar.

"No worries," Lee said. "We'll be on our way."

That was the signal for Webb. The phrase *no worries.*

Webb said to Andrews, "So it would be okay with you if we gave the reporter your name and position to verify all the other facts we are going to pass along?"

"No! I've done nothing wrong or out of the ordinary."

It seemed like the protest of someone guilty. She'd done more than just pass along information to the general who asked. Otherwise, Webb figured, she wouldn't have met them in the first place. And she was a poor actor.

"Then you'll have nothing to worry about," Lee said. "I'm sure your supervisor will see it that way too. Thanks for your time."

Lee stood. Webb stood.

Laura didn't. "Hang on. Supervisor?"

Lee remained standing, so Webb did the same. Lee had gone over this ahead of time, with Webb agreeing to follow Lee's lead.

"I'm a Vietnam vet," Lee said. "Purple Heart. Information that was leaked from your office—whether you are responsible or not—endangered my life and destroyed my property. I wanted to make this a discreet conversation to save as much trouble as possible, but apparently I'm going to have to bring in lawyers and my insurance company. They'll contact your supervisor, and I suppose fault will be determined. Along the way, it's going to make for an interesting news story."

"Sit," she said. "Sit."

She leaned forward. "I was worried about something like this. There is some information in the file that you will find interesting. If I make a copy and give it to you, what is my guarantee that you will keep my name out of this?"

"This information," Lee said. "You didn't pass it along to General Sutton, did you?"

"No," she said. "He only asked for general information and Jesse Lockewood's current address. I didn't volunteer what had been flagged. That's policy."

"If you call him back and tell him you found additional information and then give it to him, he will pass that along to the friend of a friend, and it will reach me that route and you won't be responsible for what was done with the information."

In other words, Webb thought, if she had given the information out immediately, it might have saved a trip to Washington to talk to her.

Lee eased back into his chair. As did Webb.

"That protects me," she said. "I'll have to meet you later in the day and hand you the information. Somewhere safe."

"Fair enough," Lee said. "What we also need to know is if you told anyone else besides the general about the inquiry into the files."

"No," she said. Too quickly, Webb thought. If her answer was a lie, she'd told one other person at least. The Bogeyman. Or someone who reported to the Bogeyman.

"I'm going to walk out of here without you, okay?" Laura said. "Wait at least ten minutes before you leave, so no one thinks we were together."

"One last question," Lee said. "When General Sutton made his inquiry, did he mention my name to you? Lee Knox."

"Yes," she said.

"You've been very helpful," Lee said. "Here's my number to call me when you've got the file ready."

He handed her the business card. She took it and slipped her coat on. As she left, she stopped to pay for a newspaper. Then she walked out without looking back.

"Give it a few minutes," Lee said to Webb. "Either she's legit or the Bogeyman gave her instructions to get out of here for her safety, in case we tried to use her as a hostage when he comes in. Wouldn't surprise me if she was wired for sound."

"Sure," Webb answered. He wanted to feel as calm as Lee looked.

"Trust me," Lee said. "I am as curious as you are. My bet is that someone's going to show up. Soon."

As Lee sipped on his coffee, a black Suburban with tinted windows pulled up outside the big front window of the coffee shop and parked on the sidewalk. All four doors opened, and four men in dark suits quickly stepped out.

"Finally," Lee said to Webb. "After all this time, we're about to get badged."

The four men entered the coffee shop.

"Now let's see how good your acting is," Lee whispered to Webb as the men approached and began to pull badges out of their pockets.

Lee wanted Webb to look scared.

That part was easy.

Thirty seconds later, Webb and Lee were in the Suburban. Officially in custody of the CIA.

# TWENTY-SEVEN

This was surreal for Webb. Only four days earlier, he'd been knocking on the door of a clapboard house outside Eagleville, Tennessee, a place with only one stoplight and two restaurants. Now he was sitting in the middle row of a large government SUV, two CIA men in the front, two in the back row of the eight-passenger vehicle, pulling up to the CIA headquarters in Langley, Virginia.

None of the men had spoken during the trip. Neither Webb nor Lee had asked questions.

Two men escorted them out of the Suburban and into the building between the large square pillars of a wide arch. There was beeping and scanning as the men used badges to get through the first phase of security, taking them into what looked like a semipublic concourse. Webb and Lee were searched for weapons and their devices put into lockers for safekeeping.

Deeper inside, somber men and women in dark clothing walked in determined lines across the marbled floor, their heels emitting muted clicks and thuds.

Webb and Lee crossed over the iconic seal of the CIA—a compass star imbedded in a shield with the head of an eagle, the seal itself more than three paces across.

To Webb's left was a gleaming white marble wall with five horizontal rows of stars. Webb was trying to memorize every detail of the CIA building—*the CIA!*—and had time to read the inscription above the stars: *IN HONOR OF THOSE MEMBERS OF THE CENTRAL INTELLIGENCE AGENCY WHO GAVE THEIR LIVES IN THE SERVICE OF THEIR COUNTRY.*

They passed beneath a large skylight and entered an atrium that looked like it connected a new building to an old one. Hanging above them were replicas of spy planes, painted flat black.

The CIA! Webb thought. Come on, really? The CIA!

He couldn't think of the letters without adding an exclamation point.

It gave him a sudden insight into his grandfather. This kind of thing was an adrenaline rush for Webb. The travel. The intrigue. How much more would it have been for David McLean, juggling passports and identities, flitting from country to country, all expenses paid?

The excitement of going deeper and deeper into the heart of CIA headquarters drove away most of Webb's fear, but not all of it. If they had finally been badged, they were safe, he told himself. It was the mysterious Bogeyman who was the danger. That's what he told himself.

Either way, Lee's gamble had paid off. Setting up a meeting with Laura Andrews had knocked something loose, and they were about to find out what it was.

The first of their two escorts knocked on a door, and a voice came from inside. "Come in. The door is open."

The second man opened the door and gestured for Lee and Webb to go inside. He made it clear he would be standing just outside the door with his partner. Bodyguards for whoever was inside.

Webb followed Lee.

A woman sat behind a large desk of burnished wood. The desk was bare except for some sheets of paper and a pen. She wore the obligatory serious suit. Her skin was darker than Lee's, and she was probably ten years younger. Traces of wrinkles around her eyes. A steady smile.

She stood, walked around the desk and greeted both of them with a handshake, saying, "I'm Agent Tracy Pollet. Normally, I'd start by suggesting you might be wondering why you're here, but I was able to listen in on your conversation with the woman in Veterans Affairs, so let's cut to the chase, okay? I'm interested in resolving the situation. Seriously interested."

She pointed at three comfortable leather chairs in the corner of her large office, beneath a huge framed photograph of the president. The luxury of the office and the way the chairs were set up indicated to Webb that this woman held a high position in the organization.

As they settled in the chairs, Webb said, "Hard to believe I'm here. This is the CIA. You know how many movies and TV shows I've seen with the CIA in them?"

"It's nice when they get the details right," she said with a smile. "Like whenever it shows us as the good guys."

"Good guys torch someone's house?" Lee said. "If you want to cut to the chase, why don't we get to that? My friend here might be all gaga about sitting in the office of a high-ranking CIA official, but I'm on a mission."

"It's why you wangled this invitation," she said. Another smile. "I've checked your service record. You're as smart as the reports indicate. You knew the kind of threat that would get us involved. So why did you go to the effort of getting us to bring you in?"

"Seemed easier than driving up and trying to get past security, not knowing who to talk to," Lee answered. "And by the way, I've got a friend with a video camera who recorded what happened back at the coffee shop. Got the plate numbers of the Suburban that took us out here too."

"In case we torture you and never let you out?" Tracy said, again with the hint of a smile.

"Just so you know," Lee said. "A guy loses his house, he doesn't want to take chances."

"So why don't we start there," Tracy said.

Lee crossed his legs, imitating her body language. "You heard our conversation with Laura, so you know we're trying to learn about Jesse Lockewood. There is something in his file that triggers a flag to let your organization know if anyone has interest in it. That was confirmed today when you had us picked up."

"Keep going," Tracy said.

"And when you sent someone with badges today, it confirmed something else. Someone in your organization has gone rogue on you. He—"

"Or she," Tracy said. "I'm not a fan of gender discrimination."

"I'm not a fan of any kind of discrimination," Lee said. "But it's a he."

"You can be sure of that?" She seemed amused by Lee. Almost like they were flirting. Webb realized that she and Lee weren't that far apart in age. She probably liked Lee's confidence and intelligence.

"The only person who might have a reason to go rogue is someone involved in whatever happened to Jesse Lockewood back in 'Nam," Lee said. "Lot of women in the CIA back then in Saigon?"

"Point to you," she said. "And why did getting badged today confirm that someone inside the CIA has been working on his own?"

"Let me ask you this," Lee said. "The first time the file was opened, did it ring bells here?"

"I don't explain our internal affairs," she answered.

"That means no. Because if it did, I would have been badged then instead of finding my house on fire. That tells us both that you have a rogue who wanted things taken care of without your knowledge the first time it came up. It took a phone call today from Laura Andrews to get you involved. We threatened her, so she turned to you guys. Right now, a smart woman like you is wanting to know who in your organization went rogue and why. You didn't pull us in to find out why we were interested in the file, because you already know why after wiring Laura Andrews. You pulled us in because you need our help to get the answers to both those questions. You want to know who went rogue. And why. We have the answers, if you play nice."

"He always sound this sure of himself?" she asked Webb.

"He does," Webb told her. "It gets old fast. Try spending hours in a car with him."

"You're looking for someone about my age," Lee told Tracy. "He would have been a young agent during Vietnam, and young enough to still be with the agency forty years later. So it means someone senior now, close to retirement. And that makes you nervous, because if it was someone who could keep the file hidden from you the first time it was flagged, it might be someone with more rank than you, and you have to be very careful. You need us."

"You're right," Tracy said to Webb. "It does get old fast."

She turned to Lee. "I think you're more swagger than substance. While I would be grateful if you could answer a few questions for us as a courtesy, please don't think you have any kind of leverage on the organization."

"We know where Jesse Lockewood is," Lee said. "Does that get your attention?"

She leaned forward, all amusement gone.

"Thought so," Lee said. "So if you want to find him, why don't we start with you telling us why his file was flagged?"

# TWENTY-EIGHT

Instead of answering, Tracy Pollet rose from her chair and went back to her desk.

She returned with the sheets of paper and the pen.

She read from the top sheet. "'Jim Webb. Canadian citizen. Birthplace, Toronto, Ontario. Stepfather, Elliott McLuhan Skinner, dishonorable discharge Canadian Armed Forces as a result of suspected prisoner abuse and confirmed assessment as a psychopath, according to PCL-R testing standards.'"

"Former stepfather," Webb said. "Also dishonorably discharged from marriage to my mother."

"Yet you followed in your stepfather's path," she said, still scanning the sheet. "Junior cadet for three years during your mid teens. Reached black-belt status in martial arts. Tops in marksmanship."

Tracy gazed over the top of the sheet at Webb. "You don't look military."

Lee said to Tracy, "I was liking you a lot, and still want to. Don't start making this personal, or this is going to be a lot less fun for all of us."

When she turned her gaze on Lee, Webb caught a glimpse of the steel beneath the woman's relaxed posture. "You think I'm in this job because I'm looking for fun?"

"And you think you can intimidate me?" Lee said.

They traded glares.

Webb said, "Lee, I appreciate your stepping in there for me, but if you try to fight, I think she could flip you on your butt in less than five seconds."

That was enough to break the tension.

"Not a chance," Lee said. "Ten seconds at the earliest."

Some of Tracy's frost melted. She set the top sheet aside.

"My apologies," she said to Webb. "Lee is correct. There was no need to get personal. I just wanted you to understand the resources we have here."

She tapped the other sheets. "It's important you don't underestimate my resolve. These are nondisclosure agreements. I can save you a study of the fine print. If you sign them, you are bound by the National Security Act to keep confidential everything you learn in this office. Break that confidentiality, and you will face prison terms, and I will do everything in my power to turn every asset you have into dust. When you get out of jail, you will be old and broke."

She gave them the barest of cold smiles. "Unless you sign them, we don't proceed. Are we clear on this?"

She handed each of them a sheet.

"Crystal clear," Lee said. "Dang. We could have used someone as scary as you in our platoon."

"I'll take that as a compliment."

"It was," Lee said.

Lee signed without reading the document.

So did Webb. The choice seemed simple. If he didn't sign, he wouldn't have a chance of learning whether his grandfather was innocent of being a spy and a traitor. But maybe it wasn't that simple. What if he learned the opposite?

Tracy rose again and put the papers back on her desk. Webb noticed that Lee watched her closely. Very closely. But not because he was afraid of her.

Tracy returned.

"We're happy to help," Lee said when she was back in her chair. "But now that the paperwork is out of the way, let's get a few things settled first. If you discover someone rogue from your organization torched my house, the CIA will cover the cost of rebuilding?"

It took a while, but she finally nodded.

"And you'll help this young man with his own questions?" Lee asked.

"Not so fast," she said. She turned her attention back to Webb. "I need to know how this began from your end. And what your questions are."

Webb gave Lee a questioning look.

"Son," Lee said, "now that we've brought the organization in on this for help, sooner or later they are going to find out what they want. This is the CIA. She can find out how often you change your socks, what brand of toilet paper you use and if you flush after you pee or if you're an environmentalist who prefers to let it mellow if it's yellow. If you irritate her, she can make sure you never get inside the United States again. No more Nashville music dreams for you. If you really make her mad, she'll get your friends and cousins and family dragged into it. They can be put on No Fly lists, get audited every year by whatever tax organization runs Canada."

Lee glanced at Tracy.

"Revenue Canada," she said. "Occasionally, they cooperate with us. As we do with them."

Lee said to her, "Any other kind of threat you want to throw in there to convince him he shouldn't hold back? Or did I cover everything?"

"Lasers from outer space that make your tires go flat when you're parked at the mall," she said to Webb, sounding dead serious. "New thing. We've kept it from the public. It doesn't kill anyone, but it can make life a constant pain for people."

Webb was glad she was back to good humor and joking around—at least about the lasers. And despite what Lee had just said, Webb couldn't help but think this was a pretty cool experience, all in all. This was the CIA. The CIA!

"Go ahead," Lee told Webb. "Tell her everything, from the beginning. About finding that fake Canadian passport of your grandfather's. The identification cards tucked inside."

Webb did.

When he finished, Tracy said, "We might be able to help you if you help us find the rogue. First, I need to know what you want before I agree to anything."

"Hang on," Lee told Webb. "Put on your list a green card so you can stay in the States as long as you want."

"We can make that happen if you're helpful enough," Tracy said. "But tell me what you really want."

"I want to know if my grandfather was a spy in Vietnam," Webb said, his heart thumping as if he were standing on the edge of a cliff. He dove with outstretched arms, trusting there would be a safety net for him. "I need to know if he was a good guy or a bad guy."

# TWENTY-NINE

Groups of tourists buzzed all around Webb, their whispered conversations forming bubbles of noise beneath the arch of the rotunda.

Lee was still at the hotel. Webb was in his Stampeders T-shirt again. Normally, the rotation would make this a BC Lions day. A franchise with the longest active playoff streak, the only team in the western division to have won the Grey Cup at home. Twice, of their ten. Played in Vancouver, a city at the edge of the Pacific with one of the coolest vibes in the country.

Webb didn't want a tour of the rotunda, didn't want to be part of the bubbles of noise. But he didn't have a choice. The chase was almost at an end, and it had led them to a congressman. Before he could meet with the congressman for a public-relations visit, the congressman had insisted Webb take a tour as part of "the Washington experience." The congressman had sent one of his aides to take Webb on the tour, a guy named Gerald who was barely older than Webb.

Their differences were apparent though. Webb had done his best to wash the Stampeders shirt in the hotel-room sink, but the hair dryer had wrinkled it, and on principle, Webb had refused to iron it. Maybe people ironed NFL shirts or AFL shirts, but he doubted it, and he knew for sure nobody ironed CFL shirts. In contrast, Gerald wore a navy-blue suit with a white shirt and a perfectly knotted red silk tie. Probably even the tie was ironed.

Webb's hair was in a ponytail. Gerald had dark hair in a neatly trimmed businessman's cut. Webb's ambition was to play music, even if it meant live sets in bars where people were more interested in beer than music. He guessed Gerald's ambition was to end up in administration in the White House.

The differences in their appearance didn't matter to Webb. What bothered Webb was the way Gerald acted so superior, probably because Webb wasn't dressed nicely.

But worse, they were wasting time. Webb needed to be in Congressman Nathaniel Warwick's office at exactly 2:00 PM, which was in less than fifteen minutes. But Gerald was playing tour leader in the rotunda.

"Hey, Gerry," Webb said halfway through a lecture on the series of paintings that represented important moments in American history. "How about we pretend you gave me the tour?"

Gerald sniffed. Disdain. Gerald was good at that.

"It's Gerald," Gerald said. "Not Gerry. And Congressman Warwick insisted that I give you the VIP tour."

Webb had guessed that using Gerry instead of Gerald would irritate Gerald, and he felt a twinge of guilt that he'd been correct. But two factors were in play. Webb was irritated by Gerald's air of self-importance. And Webb was nervous about what was ahead; he realized he was taking out that nervousness on Gerald.

"Gerald," Webb said, "on a scale of one to ten, with ten being the highest, how high would you rate me as a VIP here in DC? Or anywhere else in the world?"

Gerald hesitated.

"That's my point," Webb said. "Why bother with a VIP tour if I'm not a VIP?"

"Follow me," Gerald said, spinning away from the oil painting in front of them. "We'll take the tunnel to the congressman's office."

The tunnel, Gerald explained, was a wide underground hallway that allowed senators and congressmen to go directly back to their own offices after a vote, out of sight of the public.

When Webb asked if that also included getting away from journalists, Gerald's only answer was another irritated sniff, so Webb took that as a yes.

On the other end of the tunnel, they passed the guards who cleared badges for anyone headed back to the rotunda, then climbed stairs to hallways that looked and smelled as if they were part of an ancient high school.

Each congressman had a suite of offices behind wooden doors marked with their names. When they reached the door marked *Nathaniel Warwick, Congressman, Albuquerque, New Mexico,* Gerald pushed through and spoke to the secretary as if he'd just managed to sign a peace accord between Israel and Palestine.

"VIP tour completed," Gerald said. "Mr. Brandon Sayers is here for his appointment with Congressman Warwick."

The secretary was a middle-aged black woman in a nondescript green dress. "That's nice, Gerry," she said. And winked at Webb.

Gerald sniffed again and spun on his heels. Maybe he'd learned he couldn't force the woman to call him Gerald.

"Stampeders," the secretary said to Webb, smiling at the T-shirt. A name plate sat on her desk. Elizabeth. "My husband loves the CFL. How about them Eskimos, eh? Gerry, on the other hand, wouldn't know a football if it hit him in the—"

She didn't get to finish her statement.

"Welcome," a voice interrupted. "Brandon Sayers?"

Elizabeth stood, pushing back her chair as she did. She said, "Congressman Warwick, this is indeed Brandon Sayers. For your two o'clock."

Congressman Warwick walked forward, extending his hand to Webb. "It's nice to finally meet you. I know your father, of course. A good man. A very good man. I hope you enjoyed your tour."

The congressman was fit, Webb thought. Warwick was sixty-three, something Webb knew from the Warwicks' website, but he looked ten years younger. The skin on his face was tanned. And tight. Did congressmen get face-lifts?

There was a hint of gray in Warwick's sideburns. Just enough to look distinguished for television cameras. His teeth were perfect—straight and white, but not so white they looked artificial. His deep-brown suit jacket was without wrinkle.

They shook hands.

"Hello, sir," Webb said. Webb didn't see any flicker of judgment cross the congressman's face, nothing to indicate that Warwick disapproved of long hair or visitors in blue jeans and CFL T-shirts. But Webb, under the fake name, was supposed to be the son of a rich campaign supporter in New Mexico. The CIA had set it up.

"My office," Warwick said, extending his arm to the open door behind him.

Warwick paused to speak to the secretary.

"Elizabeth," he said, "make sure we get someone here with a camera for the photo op."

He aimed a perfect smile at Webb. "Leave your address with Elizabeth, and I'll make sure to sign the photo and have it framed before we mail it to you. If there's anything else I can do for you or your father, please let me know."

Another man walked into the front-office area. A man taller than Warwick, but about the same age. A man showing nicotine-stained teeth as he grimaced at Warwick with an expression that was probably supposed to be a smile, a man wearing a wrinkled black suit, peppered with dandruff or cigarette ashes or a combination of both.

Webb knew who the man was. The Bogeyman. The CIA rogue who had wanted to stop Lee and Webb but couldn't come into the open and badge them.

The Bogeyman was in the open now.

Warwick's smoothness faltered for a moment, and then he continued to escort Webb as if the other man had arrived for separate business with Elizabeth.

"Don't pretend you don't know me, Nathan," the man said from the doorway. "I need to be in on this meeting too."

The man spoke to Elizabeth. "I'm Kyle Bowden. CIA. You can put that down in the visitor book. And I'd suggest you clear whatever appointments the congressman has over the next few hours."

# THIRTY

A minute later, as all three of them settled into chairs in the congressman's office, it was obvious that Warwick had recovered. He sat in the chair behind his desk. The power position. Facing Bowden and Webb, who sat elbow to elbow on the wrong side of the desk, as if they were supplicants.

Webb noticed that his chair and Bowden's were lower than normal, making them gaze slightly upward at Warwick, who smiled at them as he rested his chin on his steepled fingers.

"Kyle Bowden," Warwick said. "I'm sorry I didn't

place your face immediately. I've seen you during some subcommittee work, right?"

"You've seen me in Vietnam," Bowden said. "When you were the captain of Jesse Lockewood's platoon, taking payments from gangsters in Saigon. The same gangsters you still have on your payroll over here. Then you blackmailed me into betraying my country and have used that leverage ever since to keep me as your CIA insider. How about let's start there?"

Warwick gave them both a tolerant, puzzled look. "Vietnam? I suppose we met there, if you say so. But I am a true patriot; therefore, your accusations are obviously false. And Vietnam was a long time ago, so forgive me for not remembering you."

Not so long, Webb thought, that Warwick wasn't against playing the soldier hero to the fullest. There were dozens of photos of him in uniform as a much younger man. Framed medallions hung on the wall. On the top shelf of the low, wide bookshelf behind the congressman's desk was some sort of bronzed base with a plaque, and on the base rested a hand grenade. Not the souvenir Webb would have chosen, but then, Webb wasn't a congressman who had served seven terms already.

"Yes, Vietnam was a long, long time ago," Bowden said. "But some things still matter after all that time. Like the military information you were passing along to the North Vietnamese through the gangster connections you had in Saigon. Like when you forced me to give up the name of a private who found out you dealt in black-market diamonds. Any of that ringing a bell?"

"I think," Warwick said, "it's time to call security."

He gave Webb an apologetic smile as he reached for his phone. "I'm sorry that you were dragged into this. I guess with an election coming up, my opponents will try anything."

"I wasn't dragged into this," Webb said. "I'm not from Albuquerque. And Aaron Sayers is not my father. That was just a way to get this appointment. My name is Jim Webb. I'm from Canada. My grandfather was David McLean. But I think you knew him in Vietnam as Sean Alexander."

There was flicker of movement across the smoothness of Warwick's face. Enough for Webb to know in his gut that everything he had learned in New Orleans from Eric McAuley was true.

"You can call security," Bowden said. "But they won't come. Not until I make the call. And then they'll be coming for you. After all these years, I'm going down, but I'm taking you with me."

"I must say," Warwick said, "all of this is crazy." He smiled. "This is one of those reality shows, right? A prank show."

"Two words," Bowden said. "Jesse Lockewood."

He nodded at Webb. Webb stood and reached into his right back pocket for a folded piece of paper, the printout of the Jesse Lockewood military ID from the photograph Webb had taken with his iPhone.

Webb unfolded it, put it on Warwick's expensive, empty desk and pushed it toward the congressman.

"Two more words," Bowden said. "Benjamin Moody."

Webb found the paper in his left back pocket and repeated the process. He watched Warwick examine the papers.

"And this means?" Warwick said.

"It means when this kid found those cards," Bowden said, "he found the only proof in the world that Jesse Lockewood had tried to get a new identity. When he photographed those cards, it meant he still had the proof no matter what happened to the cards. I told you it would be a mistake to send someone to burn down that guy's house in Tennessee. I told you it would be a mistake to send Quang Mai Loan's brother to Montgomery to try to pick up the kid from Canada. It's all caught up to us, so I cut a deal with the prosecutor. You're the big fish. They were happy to let me roll over for reduced jail time. And I'm happy to pay you back for all these years of being your lapdog. Webb is here as part of the deal too. He gets to learn about his grandfather."

"Prank," Warwick repeated. "Where are the television cameras?"

Webb was still standing.

Bowden stood too. He peeled off his suit jacket. And his shirt and pants. He stood there in baggy boxer shorts, with a sagging hairy belly, an image Webb hoped would never replay itself in his mind.

"Not wired to record any sound," Bowden said. He reached for the waistband of his boxers. "Unless you want me to pull down my—"

"No!" Warwick and Webb spoke at the same time.

Bowden began to dress.

"Webb's not wired either," Bowden said as he hitched his pants. "Webb?"

Webb peeled off his clothing down to his underwear, feeling self-conscious. He wished he had bet someone, somewhere, that he would be able to undress in a congressman's office and not get arrested or kicked out. He would have made a lot of money.

"You've made your point," Warwick said.

Webb pulled up his pants and pulled on his T-shirt.

Bowden, shirt buttoned, had taken a chair again. Webb did the same.

"Webb, tell our congressman here how it began," Bowden said. "Tell him where you got that military identification that he wanted to destroy. How you found both pieces of identification in a Canadian passport that belonged to Sean Alexander. Along with the Vietnamese identification cards that belonged to Jesse Lockewood's wife and her brother, who became a Born To Kill gangster here in the States and, like us, never stopped looking for Lockewood."

Bowden clapped his hand to his mouth in mock surprise. "Ooops. I guess I just did."

To Warwick, he said, "You know, I'm almost happy to go to jail after all these years. Words can't tell you how much I've hated you since Saigon."

"I have nothing to say," Warwick answered.

"Then I'll be happy to tell the story," Bowden said. "It begins with Jesse Lockewood seeing you in your tent one night, counting diamonds by lantern light. Remember, payment from the North Vietnamese? It's a story about Jesse agreeing to testify for the military police if they kept him safe from the gangsters. You remember, don't you? When a grunt named Casey Gardner died in action, the CIA rigged it so that Jesse Lockewood's identification went with Gardner's body, and it looked like Gardner was a deserter. Jesse Lockewood got a new military identification card as Benjamin Moody, and that was supposed to keep him safe from any assassination attempts by the gangsters. *Your* gangster friends."

"Fairy tale," Warwick said.

"Then let me remind you how someone inside the CIA tipped you off about the identity change. Someone who had major gambling debts with the same gangsters that supplied you with diamonds as payment for passing on classified military information.

Because you and I both know that the CIA operative was me. I can't tell you how much I've hated myself for letting those gangsters take Lockewood out instead of me."

"Fairy tale," Warwick repeated.

"Except the gangsters blew it when they tried to throw grenades into a taxi when Jesse was on a two-day leave in Saigon. He bailed in time and ran, and he decided maybe he wouldn't go along with a CIA offer to give him a new identity because the gangsters had found him so easily. He didn't know who he could trust at that point—at least, who he could trust among the Americans. So he went to the Canadians. Their embassy."

"Everybody loves Canadians," Webb told Warwick. "That's just a fact."

Warwick's body language suggested he didn't find Webb amusing.

"While we're having this conversation," Webb said to Bowden, "do we know yet why the Canadian embassy chose my grandfather to help Jesse and his wife escape?"

"Sure," Bowden said. "I just found out an hour ago. Our people made a few calls to your people.

Sean Alexander was the perfect person for the Canadian embassy to use. He didn't exist. You know that. Sean Alexander was just a name on a fake passport."

"It's why my grandfather had a fake passport that bothers me," Webb said. "A lot."

"To answer that, it took some serious conversations back and forth between Canada and the United States, serious conversations at a high level," Bowden answered. "In Vietnam, your grandfather was a go-between, trying to negotiate a secret peace deal. The Americans couldn't be seen even talking with the North Vietnamese. So, behind the scenes, Canadians were brought in, pretending to be businessmen. Your grandfather was not only serving Canada, but doing his part to try to help end all that bloodshed. He was given the job of making it look like Lockewood and his wife died trying to escape. He made it look so real, even Lockewood believed Sean Alexander was a traitor. But it worked. Lockewood was gone forever when he found another way to hide his identity. Except for the military cards that Sean Alexander kept, in case he needed his own protection from the CIA, there was no more record of Lockewood."

The relief was so intense, and the strain of worry so instantly vanished, that Webb felt like all the bones had been removed from his body.

"Nice stories," Warwick said. "Are we finished? Can I go back to my appointments?"

"Not yet," Bowden said. "You might want to try picking up the phone and asking Elizabeth if you have another visitor."

Warwick just frowned and shook his head. "All of this is so preposterous and without proof that I'll just sit and wait for you to leave. And if you try to spread these stories, you'll be facing libel and slander charges, and you'll lose everything you own in lawsuits."

"Fine," Bowden said. He stood and walked to the door. He opened it and waved for someone to join them.

Eric McAuley walked in. He gave a slight nod to Webb, then turned an expressionless face to Warwick.

"Warwick," Bowden said. "You remember this man, right? Once upon a time, before the CIA listed him as a dead soldier, his name was Jesse Lockewood. He's here to back up everything I just said."

# THIRTY-ONE

Webb had been hoping Warwick would react with fear or surprise at the sight of Jesse Lockewood. It would have been great to tell Lee later, so Lee could have the satisfaction of knowing what it was like for Warwick when he first realized he'd have to pay for ordering Kyle Bowden to torch Lee's house.

Instead, Warwick smiled at Jesse as if Jesse had been scheduled to appear, then held up a finger as if to say "wait just a second." This was not anything anyone in the office had expected, and in the group hesitation that followed, Warwick picked up his phone and punched a single button.

It was quiet. The ringing of the telephone at Elizabeth's desk in the outer office reached them clearly.

"Yes, Congressman," she said, her voice as audible as the ringing had been.

"I need you for a moment," Warwick said. "There's a letter that has to be mailed right away."

Again, hesitation from Webb and Bowden and Lockewood.

Elizabeth opened the door and stepped inside.

Silence from the group. Wasn't Bowden supposed to handle this? He was CIA.

Later, Webb would learn that because Bowden was a desk guy at the CIA, he didn't have much training in combat operations. Lockewood had thought it was Bowden's operation, so he wasn't about to lead on this, and Webb had thought the same thing. So because Bowden hadn't acted, neither had Webb or Lockewood.

"Here's the letter," Warwick said, reaching into his drawer.

That's when it occurred to Webb that Warwick might pull out a pistol. That's the way it happened in the movies.

But Warwick brought up a white envelope and waited for Elizabeth to cross the office for it.

She frowned. Obviously, she felt the tension but had no idea what was going on.

Bowden didn't stop her. So neither did Webb or Lockewood.

She stepped around the desk. Warwick held out the envelope. As she reached for it, he grabbed her wrist, spun her around and pulled her toward him.

He wrapped his other arm around her neck and put her in a chokehold, using her body as a shield. As she gagged, with his free hand he groped behind him for the top of the bookshelf.

No way, Webb thought, as his mind made the connection. No way.

Webb's body seemed to go into action with only one conscious thought.

He's going for the hand grenade.

The large, expensive desk was a barrier between them. Webb launched himself over it, but it was too late.

Warwick had managed to close his fingers over the hand grenade and pull it loose from its base. At the same time, he brought a knee up and rammed it into Webb's chest as Webb's upper body slid across the desk.

It stopped Webb's momentum, and he grunted in pain. His body was spread across the desk as Warwick twisted sideways with Elizabeth still in his grip. Warwick brought the hand with the grenade around in front of her, which left his left hand free to pull the pin from the grenade.

It was a small sound. A slight tick of metal against metal.

A sound that seemed as large as the impact of a freight train.

Warwick dropped the pin as everyone froze. Including Webb on the top of the desk.

"It's given me great satisfaction over the years," Warwick said in a conversational tone, "knowing I've had a live grenade to use any time I wanted to. I can't tell you how many times I wanted to lob it into a crowd of idiotic journalists."

Elizabeth was choking.

"I'll ease off the pressure," he told her, "but if you try anything, I'll crush your throat. Understand?"

Elizabeth grunted and he gave her some air. Then he looked at Webb.

"Get off the desk. You look ridiculous there."

Webb felt ridiculous too, as he rolled over sideways to land on his feet at the far edge.

"Now," Warwick told them, "first tell me I'll never get away with this."

"We came in while you were gone for lunch and bugged your office," Bowden said. "This meeting was set up so you'd incriminate yourself. I'd say you've done a good job of that. We've got our guys waiting in the hallway."

"Doesn't that feel better?" Warwick said to Bowden. "Elizabeth and I are going for a walk. It's nice that the office is bugged. Whoever is listening in on this will know that as long as I've got a good grip on the grenade, she's safe. If something happens to me and I drop it, she'll die with me. So if you have snipers in place, they won't do any good. She's going to stay with me until both of us are away from the office. I want a cab waiting on the street for us, and she's going to stay with me until I'm on my private jet."

Webb thought he understood the danger of the grenade, but it wasn't until he looked it up later that he found out how an armed grenade goes off, second by second.

*Squeeze the strike lever against the grenade. Pull the pin. Throw the grenade. The spring-loaded lever pops away from the body of the grenade. As the lever pops away, it throws the striker down on a percussion cap inside the grenade, throwing a tiny spark. The spark ignites a slow-burning fuse. Four seconds later, the delay material burns through. Detonator explodes. The primary explosion of the detonator sets off a secondary, much larger explosion around the sides of the grenade. The fragmented pieces of the body of the grenade create a shower of shrapnel moving at the speed of bullets, an outward-expanding ball of death like a shotgun blast.*

Elizabeth either didn't know about this or was too mad to care. And, as Webb would also find out later, she'd been taking self-defense lessons.

She wasn't a small woman, and with a backward punch that barely missed her right ear, she popped Warwick in the nose with the square of her knuckles. At the same time, she stomped down with her heel on his instep. Any crunch of the small bones in Warwick's foot was lost in a howl of pain as blood spurted from his nose.

He lost his grip on her neck, and she turned around and kneed him in the groin.

The grenade rolled loose. To Webb's feet.

A dozen thoughts ripped through his mind: Throw it out the window. No, what if the glass doesn't break? No, what if the glass breaks and it explodes on the sidewalk and kills people outside on the street? Okay then. Jump on it. Die a hero. No, who wants to die? How about shove Warwick on it so that his body takes the explosion? Yes! Hang on—no, that would be murder.

All those thoughts took maybe two seconds to process, in a blur where Webb was going more on instinct than consideration. But there he was, holding a live grenade in his right hand, with Bowden and Lockewood diving for cover.

Corner, he thought. Filing cabinet.

Webb took two steps and rolled the grenade across the top of the filing cabinet; it fell into the corner behind the cabinet. Then he dove behind the desk, where Bowden and Lockewood were already piled on each other. It was a soft landing, with Bowden taking most of it.

Everyone decided later that the filing cabinet probably would have been thick enough to absorb the blast. Filled with papers, it would have been like a metal-encased barrier with the equivalent of dozens of telephone books serving as padding. Everyone decided later that Webb had reacted superbly under the circumstances. And that he would have been a hero.

Except the seconds ticked by. Four. Five. Six. Seven. Eight...

Without a blast.

Webb closed his eyes and held them closed. It felt great to be alive. Really, really great. With that realization, he felt some of his internal darkness slide away. He opened his eyes again. From his position on top of Bowden's body, Webb saw that Warwick was lying on his stomach on the floor, moaning, one hand on his nose, his other hand clutching his groin.

The grenade had not exploded. Elizabeth kicked Warwick in the butt. Hard. Enough to change the moan to a yelp.

"I've always wanted to do that," she said.

Then she glared at Webb and Bowden and Lockewood as they untangled themselves and pushed themselves to their feet.

"Fools," she said. "Buying into his bluff like that. The jerk has never spoken a word of truth in his life, so why believe him about the grenade? And even he's not stupid enough to keep a live grenade in his office.

Not when children come in all the time for photo opportunities."

Bowden leaned over, hands on his knees, and tried to draw more air into his lungs. Definitely not a field operative.

"Hope your nose is broken," Elizabeth said to Warwick, and she kicked him again in the meat of his butt. She kept kicking Warwick until the security people arrived to rescue him from her.

# THIRTY-TWO

The Bluebird Cafe was in a strip mall outside of downtown Nashville. Maximum capacity, ninety music fans. It was Monday night, singer-songwriter night, and Webb was one of those ninety filling it to capacity. Lee Knox, at the small table beside him, was another.

The interior of the café was as ordinary as the outside. Bunch of tables, square-back chairs. The stage, which was a generous name for it, was more like an open spot in the center of the tables. Musicians on the stage could reach out and touch the crowd, half of which was directly behind them.

What made it out of the ordinary was the music. There was something so organic about stepping out on the tightrope, playing music live, Webb thought. Nothing polished. Plenty of mistakes. No producer to bail you out and auto-tune your vocals.

It was the break time, halfway through the sets.

"They all sounded good," Lee said, leaning back. "Thanks for the invite. I'm enjoying this."

There was only one person Webb had wanted to invite to this evening. Lee Knox.

Lee said, "Sorry I was a little late. I wanted to give this to you right away, but the music had started."

He slid an envelope across the table. "From the insurance company. Told you they might pay a fee if we could prove liability on someone else."

Webb wanted to open the envelope, but he played it cool.

"Thanks," Webb said.

"Enough there to get you through six months, at least," Lee said. "You got your green card, right? You don't have to hurry back to Canada?"

"Tracy delivered," Webb said.

"Good," Lee said. "I have a buddy with a houseboat here in Nashville. He's looking for someone to stay on it while he's away, make sure everything's all right."

"Houseboat. Nashville."

"Sounds crazy, I know. But there's this spot on the river. About twenty houseboats. Got a good vibe. You'll like it. Save you a bunch on rent too."

Webb let out a deep breath. This was good news. No, GREAT news. He wasn't going to give up on trying to get his songs back from the producer who had ripped him off, but this money would give him a chance to try cutting more songs with a new producer. Still, despite the good news, he was nervous.

"Hey! Mile 112,'" Lee said. "That's easy to remember."

Lee was talking about the poster. Webb couldn't put his own name up on the poster with the other singer-songwriters. There was another Jim Webb, really famous in the music business. Wouldn't look good and would be too confusing.

"Mile 112," Webb repeated. "Just me right now— no band. That trip up north for my grandfather? Mile markers all along the way. That's where I got the name. Mile 112 was at Devil's Pass. Significant place for me. I told you about that, driving back from DC."

That was when Webb had told Lee about his step-father. About the grizzly attack. About the depression he faced every day, and the lack of appetite and the anger. It was also when Webb discovered that Lee had been telling the truth. Getting that stuff out, sharing it with a friend, was the first step to making it better. That realizing it was there, like a broken leg or broken arm, helped a person start healing inside.

Lee nodded. "Come up with any good songs of your own for mile oneTwelve?"

"Working on it," Webb said. "But nothing so far that I know is good. Nothing my gut tells me is the one. Nothing that's going to set me apart. I'm here because I want to practice playing in front of a crowd."

"Scared?"

"Puckered up so bad you wouldn't believe it," Webb said. "This *is* the Bluebird."

"Advice?" Lee said. "Can I give you some?"

"Sure."

"Don't rush it. You get up there, let some silence hang. Nervous people fill the silence, and nervous people make the crowd nervous."

The lights flashed on and off, a signal for people to start making their way back to their tables.

"You making any trips to Montgomery in the next while?" Lee asked, as if he knew changing the subject would help Webb get through the nervousness.

"Why would I do that?" Webb said.

"Ali."

"Well then," Webb said. "Maybe."

"Like maybe the sun is going to rise in the east tomorrow morning," Lee said.

"You making any trips to DC in the next while?" Webb said.

"Why would I do that?" Lee asked.

"Tracy. At the CIA. I noticed you spent time closely inspecting her every time she couldn't catch you looking."

"Needed to know if she was carrying a weapon," Lee said. "Just basic intelligence work."

"And was she?"

"Don't know," Lee said. "That would take a trip back to DC, wouldn't it?"

Webb laughed, glad for something to relieve the tension.

"Lee," he said. "I found out something about Sinatra. Couldn't wait to tell you about it. That movie, *Ocean's Eleven*?"

"Yeah?"

"I did some research. Found out it was filmed in the casinos in Las Vegas back when a lot of casinos wouldn't let blacks through the door. Sinatra's friend, Sammy Davis Jr., he was black."

"Yeah?" Some hesitation in Lee's answer.

"Sinatra put the word out. He wouldn't go in a casino unless they let Sammy in with him. Even went further than that. Did some stage acts with Sammy, poking fun at segregation. How you feel about that? Was Sinatra hip or square?"

Lee looked away, as if he was studying the posters on the walls of the famous musicians who had performed at the Bluebird.

He finally looked back at Webb. "How I feel is that maybe I should have stopped to learn about this before making assumptions about someone I didn't know."

Rueful smile as Lee continued. "And how I feel is that the inability to let go of crap exists in all colors. And it feels good, when you do let it go."

A guy with a nose ring walked up. The sound guy. "Dude, you're next. Need help plugging in?"

"I'm good," Webb said. "Thanks."

Webb stood.

"Haircut," Lee said from his chair. "Looks good on you."

No more ponytail.

"I lost some heavy baggage that I didn't need to carry anymore," Webb said. "Like you said, the inability to let go of crap exists in all colors. Glad I finally let go. My stepfather has nothing on me now."

As he took the chair behind the mike, he caught Lee's grin. That felt good too.

Webb plugged in his guitar, strummed it a few times. He'd thought of telling Lee that the first song was for him, but Lee would figure it out. Or he wouldn't. If Webb had to explain it, it would lose something for both of them.

Webb was ready, his heart pounding hard against his ribs when the lights went down, except for the spotlight on him and his J-45 guitar and his Montreal Alouettes T-shirt. This wasn't the time to explain to the crowd that the Alouettes were once the Baltimore Stallions, and that the franchise ignored that inconvenient part of team history.

Webb smiled out at the spotlights, which hurt his eyes. Couldn't see anything except the lights. He made himself silently count to four.

"Hey, everybody," Webb said. He forced himself to speak slowly. With confidence he didn't feel. "It's an honor to be here at the Bluebird. I thought I'd start by saying I learned something lately from a friend. I love party songs, but once in a while we need a song that means something."

Silence. Ominous silence. Of a crowd bracing itself for yet another singer-songwriter who took himself way too seriously.

"Unfortunately," Webb said, "no matter how hard I try, I can't come up with that song."

Laughter. Good laughter. As if suddenly the crowd had decided to like him.

That's when Webb knew it was going to turn out all right, him and his guitar here at the Bluebird Cafe.

"So," Webb said, "if you can get past the folksy beginning, I'll play you something you might already know. It's from the seventies. My contribution is that I've changed up the tune a bit. I like the song because it reminds me that in the end, it's good to be good to each other. No matter what differences we have. We all have more in common with each other than things that set us apart. And we pay too high a price when we forget that simple truth."

Like a congressman led out from his office in handcuffs, because money meant more to him than the lives of American soldiers.

"Amen," someone yelled out. "Amen, brother!"

The guy had probably had too much beer, but Webb grinned at the applause that followed the enthusiastic outburst.

"Yes, sir," Webb said. "I'd be happy to call you brother."

With the crowd expectant, he waited five seconds to build some tension. Then he hit the first notes on his guitar. Softly. Made people lean in to catch what he was playing. Then he picked up the volume to give the guitar riffs momentum.

There were whistles of appreciation. Even with the chords changed to a dark minor, they now knew exactly where he was going. And wanted more.

Webb leaned into the mic for the vocals and sang the opening words. *Listen, children to a story / that was written long ago / 'bout a kingdom on a mountain / and the valley folk below…*

As he sang, Webb couldn't help but think about Jesse Lockewood, wanting only a quiet life with his wife and family, finding a way to survive all that had been horrible about Vietnam. About Casey Gardner, and how his family had been overjoyed to learn Casey wasn't a deserter, but a war hero. About his grandfather David McLean, taking risks under an assumed name, knowing there would be no public reward for the help he could give and the risk of death if he failed. About Lee Knox, doing what he could, under the radar, to make things better. Lee wasn't a perfect man; like everyone, he had his biases, but he cared, and in the end, that did matter. Webb thought about himself, and how good it had felt to cut his hair and get out of the prison he'd put himself in.

By the time Webb got to the final chorus, everyone in the Bluebird was standing and singing with him, so he had no choice but to stand with his guitar, ignore the mic and blend his voice in with all of them.

*There won't be any trumpets blowing come the judgment day. On the bloody morning after, one tin soldier rides away.*

# ACKNOWLEDGMENTS

Many thanks to my editor, Sarah Harvey, for pushing me to make Webb's story the best it could possibly be. And thanks to the rest of the amazing Orca team who do so much behind the scenes to make the series successful. I'd also like to acknowledge the passion and dedication of teachers Cheryl Kennedy, Heather Earl, Allison Boyd and Gwen Dermott-Ainscough, whose students were the test readers who offered me much-needed feedback on the first and second drafts of the novel. And thanks to those great students. You guys rock.

SIGMUND BROUWER is the bestselling author of numerous books for children and adults, including *Rock & Roll Literacy* and titles in the Orca Echoes, Orca Currents and Orca Sports series. *Tin Soldier* is the sequel to *Devil's Pass*—Sigmund's first novel in Seven (the series), which was a finalist for the John Spray Mystery Award, a Red Maple nominee and a *Kirkus Reviews* Critics' Pick. Visit www.rockandroll-literacy.com for information on Sigmund's school presentations. Sigmund's website for readers is at www.rockandrollbooks.com. Find Webb's music, inluding his remake of "One Tin Soldier" at iTunes under mile oneTwelve. Sigmund and his family divide their time between his hometown of Red Deer, Alberta, and Nashville, Tennessee.

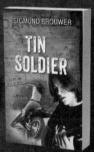

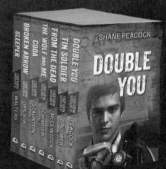

# DISCOVER ANOTHER EXCITING BOOK IN THE
# SEVEN SEQUELS

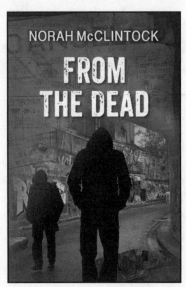

9781459805378  $10.95 PB
9781459805392  EPUB
9781459805385  PDF

Rennie is in Uruguay when his cousins discover some unsettling items at their dead grandfather's cottage. Rennie's mission: find out whether the old man was a spy and a traitor, and if he helped a Nazi war criminal escape justice.

# NINE

I'm covered in blood after my attempted CPR. I'm still shaking. The ambulance guys check me out. They wrap me in a blanket because I'm shaking so hard. They inspect me for wounds. They listen to my heart a couple of times. Apparently, it's racing. They tell me it's shock at what I've witnessed. Once they're satisfied I'm not hurt, they hand me over to the cops, who take me back to a police station, put me into a small room and tell me to take a seat, that someone will be with me shortly. If I'm suspected of anything or under arrest, no one bothers to tell me. I'm not worried—not yet anyway. I haven't done anything.

Besides, down here the cops have to tell you whether you're arrested or not. If they don't and the case goes to trial, it will get kicked because they didn't follow the rules. But they fingerprinted me, which I don't understand. Why the fingerprints if I'm not under arrest? I guess I could have said no. But, like I said, I haven't done anything. If you haven't broken any laws, you have no worries, right?

So I sit—or try to—and I wait. I'm as squirmy as an addict in need of a top-up. I still can't believe what happened. I don't want to believe it. I stand again, and I pace. I stop for a few seconds to look at the mirror on one wall. Of course, I know it's not really a mirror. It's a one-way window. Whoever is on the other side can see me, and that's all I can see too. Me. With blood on the front of my jacket. With a face that looks too white considering how much surf and sun I've had lately.

Me, pacing. Which makes me look guilty of something. But I can't stop. I don't even want to think about sitting still. I just want out.

The door opens and a massive black guy comes into the room. He tells me his name— Daniel Carver—and says he's a homicide detective.

He's wearing a dark suit with a shirt and tie, and he's carrying a file folder. He flashes me his badge and tells me to take a seat.

"I didn't do anything," I tell him. That doesn't sound right. I don't want him to get the wrong idea. "I mean, I tried CPR. But it was too late." There, that's better. Sort of.

"I said sit." He doesn't yell it at me. It sounds more like a guy giving a command to his dog. And like a good dog—or like someone who knows enough about cops to know it's not a good idea to annoy them, not when something this serious has happened—I sit. But one of my legs is jumping up and down like it's keeping time to music that no one can hear. Carver notices. He looks at it. I make it stop. Carver looks me in the eye. My leg starts to jump again.

"Rennie Charbonneau. That's your name?" He's got the deepest voice I've ever heard and a way of talking like I'm a piece of garbage he's about to ditch as soon as he can find out who tossed me in his path. He scares me more than the Major ever has, and that's rare. I don't get scared very often, and I sure don't get intimidated. Maybe it's shock, like the ambulance guy said. "That's a French name, right?"

I nod. "My dad's Quebecois." Will a Detroit cop know what that is? "He's from Quebec. It's in Canada."

"I know where Quebec is," Carver says mildly. He's looking at a page inside the file folder. "What's a Canadian boy from Quebec doing down here in Detroit over Christmas, Rennie?"

I start to relax, even though I know I probably shouldn't. Just because a cop—a homicide cop, at that—sounds friendly, it doesn't mean he is. More than likely he's trying to find out what I sound like and look like and how I act when I'm not being grilled and not spinning a web of lies. He's using psychology on me. I tell myself to relax. I remind myself of something I've heard the Major say before, which is that you might be able to put one over on a good investigator now and then, but unless you're a career criminal—a *successful* career criminal—you're basically a rookie up against someone who's seen and heard it all. Carver is doing his job here, the same job he's been doing for a couple of decades, judging by the look of him. Me—I'm just in a situation that I sincerely hope is temporary.

"I'm on my way home from a vacation with my dad," I say.

He glances up from the folder. "Oh? He's here with you?"

"No, sir."

He hears the "sir," and a wolflike smile appears on his face.

"You trying to snow me, Rennie?"

"No, sir."

His eyes lock onto mine. If I look hard enough, I can see his vision of my future in their black depths. I want to look away, but I know not to. If you don't look straight at the cops when they're talking to you, they start to think you're lying. And if you're lying, then you're probably guilty of something. But what I said is true. For once I'm not trying to snow anyone with the "sir." It's just that Carver reminds me of the Major, so the "sir" is an automatic reflex.

"My dad shipped out," I tell him. Then, before he can ask, I add, "He's with the military. He has an assignment overseas. Afghanistan."

"And you?"

"Me?"

"You haven't explained what you're doing in Detroit. It says here you're a Canadian citizen, residing in Canada. You have friends here?"

"No, sir."

He looks at the file folder again. "You told the officers on the scene that you had dinner with friends and that you were in the alley where the shooting occurred because you were doing a favor for one of those friends."

I feel my leg jump. I wish it wouldn't, but I can't stop it. I realize it looks like he's caught me in a lie. But it's not a lie. The fact is, I can barely remember what I told the two uniforms who questioned me at the scene. Mostly I was thinking how close I'd just come to being a corpse like Duane. If those cops were to walk into the room right now, I doubt I'd recognize them. There are only two faces burned into my brain, and believe me, I wish they weren't. They're Duane after he stopped breathing and the guy with the massive spider tattoo.

"They aren't really friends," I tell Carver. "I mean, I didn't know any of them until the day before yesterday. They're more like acquaintances."

Carver shakes his head. He's disappointed. "It's late, Rennie, and it's been a long day. Let's not play word games, okay?"